MW01102235

Gallop for Gold

Sharon Siamon

Illustrations by Frances Clancy

James Lorimer & Company, Publishers
Toronto, 1992

To Beryl

James Lorimer & Company Ltd. acknowledges with
thanks the support of the Canada Council, the Ontario
Arts Council and the Ontario Publishing Centre in the
development of writing and publishing in Canada.

All illustrations: Frances Clancy

Canadian Cataloguing in Publication Data
Siamon, Sharon
  Gallop for gold.

(A Lorimer blue kite adventure)

 ISBN 1-55028-381-2 (bound). ISBN 1-55028-380-4
(pbk.)

I. Title. II. Series.
PS8587.I33G35 1992 jC813'.54 C92-093761-6
PZ7.S42Ga 1992

James Lorimer & Company, Publishers
Egerton Ryerson Memorial Building
35 Britain Street
Toronto, Ontario
M5A 1R7

Printed and bound in Canada

Contents

1	It's Got to Be Gold	1
2	Only the Best for Remington Wickers	6
3	Remington Is Dumped	12
4	Remington the Raccoon	18
5	Berries and Gold	24
6	Invitation to Adventure	35
7	Remington Shows Off	42
8	Get Me Out of Here!	50
9	Kiff to the Rescue	57
10	Remington Makes Toast	65
11	Kiff Battles Beavers	72
12	Remington Gets a Lesson	80
13	Bear Falls	88
14	Kiff's Secret	92
15	Riding Lessons	98
16	Disaster!	107
17	The Mysterious K.K.	113
18	Remington Tries	120
19	Race to Camp Saddlemore	125
20	Stuck in the Muck	132
21	Stop the Slimes!	137
22	Beavers and Mr. Mountjoy	142
23	Norse Horse Expert	147
24	The Last Ride	154

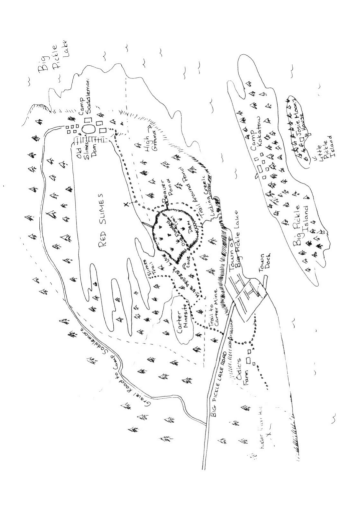

1

It's Got to Be Gold

"Not *another* million-dollar gold rock," Josie Moon moaned. "Kiff, you are so boring! We can never just go for a ride. You're always hopping off your horse and picking up another lump of fool's gold. Which is not surprising, since you are a FOOL!"

"Okay, Moonface." Kiff Kokatow gripped Smoke's reins in one hand and scooped up the rock in his other. "Maybe some of the other rocks were fool's gold. But look! Look at this little speck right here..." He held up the rock so Josie and his friend Odie Pedersen could see it clearly. His brown eyes danced with excitement. "Fool's gold sparkles. This gleams. Fool's gold is hard crystals. This is so soft I can scratch it with my nail."

He dropped Smoke's reins to demonstrate and Smoke stood patiently. Her saddle bags already bulged with the rock samples Kiff had picked up exploring the old Carter gold mine. Since the three friends had got horses the summer before, they had explored many old roads like the one that led to the Carter Mine.

"Poor Smoke," Josie burst out, as Kiff lovingly stowed this rock with the rest. "She's going to get a swayback carrying your stupid old rocks!"

"This one's real gold, I'm telling you. And someday, I'll be rich, and you'll just be poor old, broke old, Josephine Moon," Kiff teased. He threw his leg over Smoke's back and swung himself up into the saddle. "C'mon. There's a huge open pit just over here. They say it has no bottom."

"As long as we keep moving," Josie muttered to herself. She wheeled her horse, Skydive, into position behind Smoke once more.

Rocks clattered under the horses' hooves. Josie, Kiff and Odie caught glimpses of the old ruined walls of the gold mine through the young trees that had grown up around it.

"The pit is just ahead." Kiff urged Smoke forward.

Just then three long blasts of a car-horn echoed in the distance.

HONK!...HONK!...HONK!

Kiff pulled up his reins with a jerk. "Oh, no! I forgot," he groaned.

HONK!...HONK!...HONK!

The car-horn blared again. It was coming from the direction of the town of Big Pickle Lake, half an hour down the trail behind them.

Three long honks was a well-known signal around the lake. It meant guests had arrived for the fishing camp that Kiff's parents ran on Big Pickle Island. Since the only way to get to the island was by boat, visitors parked at the public dock in town and blew their horns three times. Then Kiff's boat, the *Queen*, came across the lake to pick them up.

Odie looked at Kiff with a puzzled frown. "Are you expecting somebody at the camp?" he asked. Kiff had already wheeled Smoke around on the trail back to town.

"The Wickers are coming," Kiff nodded. "I was supposed to be at the dock to meet them. Wouldn't you know old Remington would show up just when I was doing something important!" He urged Smoke into a fast trot.

"Remington Wickers?" Josie raced after him. "How long is he staying this time?" Two summers before, Remington and his family had spent a memorable month at Camp Kokatow.

"He isn't staying!" Kiff shouted back. "Not that it's any of your business, Moonbrain. He's just dropping in to say hello."

"But they live six hundred kilometres away!" Josie shook her head. "That's a long way to drive, just to drop in, Kiff."

HONK!...HONK!...HONK!

The horn was louder, more impatient this time.

"I *hope* he isn't staying," Kiff muttered to himself. Ever since the Wickers had called on their car-phone to say they were on their way from St. Catharines, Kiff had had a horrible feeling that Remington was about to destroy another of his summers. Just when he was on the verge of making a big gold discovery. But I'll get back up here, he promised himself, Remington or no Remington!

"Old Remington..." Odie rode up beside him. "Remember how scared he was of bloodsuckers?" He laughed. "Remember how he hollered when he got one on his toe? 'HELP, THEY'RE SUCKING MY BLOOD! I'M DYING!' " He imitated Remington's screech.

"Don't remind me," Kiff groaned. "What a wimp! C'mon, Odie. The faster we get down to the dock, the faster the Wickers will be on their way." A few minutes later they had crossed the main road and were on the wider trail that led to the town of Big Pickle Lake.

"I wonder what Remington looks like now?" Josie rode up on Kiff's other side.

"Skinny and white," Kiff shouted. "Watery eyes, drippy nose. Hopeless! That's how he'll look. He almost drove me crazy last time, following me around the camp. I'll bet he hasn't changed a bit."

"Well, we'll soon know," Odie panted. They pulled their horses to a halt on the hill overlooking the town dock and the dirt landing where boaters parked their cars and trucks. "There's the Wickers' truck. Holey pyjamas, what are they hauling?"

Down below, on the landing, along with all the battered pickups and RV's, was a shiny white four-by-four. Behind it, they could see a trailer, shaped like a loaf of white bread.

Josie Moon leaned forward in her saddle. Her dark eyes were gleaming. She shook her dark hair back from her forehead. "I know what that is," she said. "That's a horse van."

2

Only the Best for Remington Wickers

"A horse van!" Kiff snorted. "What would the Wickers be doing with that?"

"Hauling a horse, probably," Josie said calmly.

"You must be out of your moony little mind. Why would they bring a horse up here?"

"Where's their big boat?"Odie said. The last time the Wickers had arrived at the landing, they were towing a huge fishing boat, the *Salmon Snatcher*.

"Come on," Kiff said. "Let's ride down and find out." At the bottom of the hill, they left the three horses tethered at the side of the parking lot and walked towards the Wickers' truck. As they got closer, the door flew open and out stepped Remington. Odie, Kiff and Josie stopped dead in their tracks.

Remington was wearing a black velvet helmet with a chin strap. His jacket was red and fit him like a glove. Below the jacket, he wore brown riding breeches which stuck out on both sides of his legs, and below that, shiny black boots. With the boots on, he was almost as tall as Josie Moon. Only a few wisps of white-blond hair sticking out from under his riding helmet told them that this was the Remington they knew.

"Hello." His pale eyes swept past them to the sparkling lake and the dark green shore of Big Pickle Island in the distance. "It still looks the same," he said. "Are those your horses?" Remington's voice hadn't grown to fit his new taller body. It was still whiny and demanding.

"Yup," Kiff finally nodded.

Remington slapped his riding crop against his breeches and marched off to inspect the horses.

At this moment, Mrs. Wickers gushed forward. She, at least, looked exactly the way they remembered her — as shiny and white as her truck. She was so perfect, she could have been sprayed with plastic. "And here are all your little friends to meet you. How nice," she called to Remington's disappearing back. He was still heading for the horses.

Then Mr. Wickers levered himself out from behind the truck's steering wheel and strode towards them. He was tall, and large around the middle, and wore a Blue Jays cap. "Well, isn't this great!" he grinned. "How's the fishing?"

By now Remington had reached the horses. Dinah, Odie's brown mare, tried to poke a friendly nose in his pocket. Remington jerked away. He backed off from the three horses so fast he almost tripped over his boots.

"What breed are those three horses?" he panted as he reached the truck. "I haven't seen anything like them on my horse videos."

"Oh, they're a special Northern breed," Kiff said, making this up as he went along. "You won't find them on any videos. Too rare." He gazed at Remington. "Speaking of rare...can I ask you a question? What is that...costume you're wearing?"

"Riding clothes, of course," Remington sniffed. "I'm on my way to a riding camp. Naturally, they expect you to arrive properly dressed."

Kiff's eyes got very narrow.

"Doesn't Remington look wonderful?" Mrs. Wickers asked. "When he heard you had all got horses last summer, well... He just wouldn't let us alone until he had a horse of his own."

"You kids sure do think alike!" Mr. Wickers shook his head and laughed. "Remington has himself a rare breed, too. Icelandic." He gestured towards the trailer.

Josie stared at the horse van. "You have an Icelandic horse, in there? You're taking your horse...to camp?"

"Of course!" said Mrs. Wickers. "There's the most marvelous equestrian camp — that means

8

riding, dear — just *minutes* from here. Camp Saddlemore. Run by the *best* people...the Mountjoys, of New York."

Remington interrupted. "Let me tell it, Mother. I'm going to be training for the New York Horse Show. So, naturally I have to have my horse, Efstur, with me."

"*Efstur*?" Kiff said. "That's your horse's name?"

"It means 'The Best' in Icelandic." Mrs. Wickers looked as though she would burst with pride. "We're just sure that Remington and Efstur will win a gold medal in the junior class."

"Would you kids like to see him?" Mr. Wickers boomed.

From inside the horse van came a burst of impatient whickering. WUNH-HA WUNH-HA-WUNH!

"Yes. Let's get him out," Josie said quickly. "The poor horse must be tired of being cooped up in the van."

Remington glanced nervously at the van. "I don't want to let him out...here," he said. "It would be better to wait until we get to the camp where they have proper facilities."

Kiff snorted under his breath. "Proper facilities, my armpit." What could be better than the Big Pickle Lake landing? Here, a horse had clean water to drink, lots of fresh air, smooth dirt underfoot and plenty of space to move around. Remington Wickers was a snob.

"Don't forget we have to slip over to Camp Kokatow and get that paper signed," Mrs. Wickers reminded her husband. "Look. Kiffy's boat is coming to get us!" She marched off towards the dock.

What piece of paper? And how dare she call him *Kiffy*! Kiff was bad enough as a nickname, but *Kiffy*! Kiff had the greatest urge to plant a dusty footprint on the back of Mrs. Wickers' clean white pants as he followed her down to the dock.

"Well," Mr. Wickers shrugged, "looks like we have a boat to catch, Remington. But you're welcome to open the back of the horse van and take a good look at the little fellow," he told Josie and Odie.

The *Queen* was cutting a smooth curve through the blue water to approach the dock. She had a red-and-white striped awning on top and silver aircraft floats on the bottom. Kiff's twin huskies, Tiska and Miska, sat in the bow, their ears blowing back in the wind. They sat as straight and proud as two dog statues. It was their job to welcome each new guest to the island.

"Ugh!" Remington shuddered. "I remember those dogs. I hate them."

Kiff twitched with a sudden desire to shove Remington into Big Pickle Lake. He caught the line his father threw and looped it around a cleat in the dock.

"Want to take the wheel?" his dad called, as the Wickers went aboard.

"Sure..." Any other time, Kiff would have felt proud to pilot the big *Queen*. But now, he just wanted to stay with Odie and Josie and the horse van. He'd take a horse — even with a dumb name like *Efstur* — over the Wickers family any day! Kiff couldn't believe how much money they had to spend. Two years ago, they'd bought thousands of dollars worth of fishing gear, just so Remington could win the Big Pickle Lake fish derby. Now it was horses.

But what, Kiff wondered, did the Wickers want at Camp Kokatow? He had to find out!

3

Remington Is Dumped

What the Wickers wanted was unbelievable!

They were all sitting in the main lodge at Camp Kokatow. Kiff and his parents sat on one side of the long wood table that ran down the centre of the lodge. The Wickers perched on the bench on the other side.

They wanted Kiff's parents to sign a long, official-looking piece of paper. It promised that they would be responsible for Remington while the Wickers went off on a six-week cruise!

"Where did you say you were going?" Kiff's dad looked puzzled.

"It's an Eco-cruise to the Rain Forests — " Mrs. Wickers waved her hand " — Costa Rica and beyond."

"Six weeks exploring the world's wonders," Mr. Wickers beamed across the table at Kiff's father.

The Wickers were the world's wonders, Kiff thought. He tried to imagine what his parents were going to say.

"Well, it's an awfully big responsibility..." his mother started.

"But Remington will be at Camp Saddlemore the whole time," Mrs. Wickers broke in quickly. "He'll be absolutely no trouble."

Remington was staring out the lodge window, as if this conversation had nothing to do with him.

"We thought, since you were so handy to the riding camp, you'd be the ideal folks," Mr. Wickers said. Then he sighed. "If we hadn't paid megabucks for those Eco-cruise tickets, I'd stay right here at Camp Kokatow and fish." He looked longingly around the comfortable lodge with its high, open ceiling and stone fireplace.

"But our trip is all booked," Mrs. Wickers said firmly. "And it may be our last chance to see all those endangered species. We can come back here, any time." She waved the paper at Kiff's mother. "I'm sure nothing's going to happen, but the camp requires someone to call in an emergency."

I'll bet no one else would sign for old Remington, Kiff thought. Who would want him? He looks like a lawn ornament standing there in those riding clothes! Two years ago Remington's

parents had dumped him on Kiff while they went fishing. Now he was old enough to dump at a riding camp!

Kiff could see his own parents exchange glances. What could they say, with Remington right there?

"Well, I suppose it will be all right," Kiff's mother reached for the pen. "Just be sure to write down how we can get in touch with you."

Mr. Wickers dug out a shiny white business card from his wallet. "We'll be off in the Rain Forest most of the time," he boomed cheerfully. "Pretty hard to reach. But my office can always get me. They handle all my property management."

Remington sighed, as if he was used to being just another chunk of property. Then he picked up Kiff's father's best fishing rod from a shelf and pretended to cast with it. He snagged the saltshaker on the long dining table. It fell with a clatter and spilled salt.

Kiff's parents signed. Mrs. Wickers flipped the signed paper into her bag. "Well, I suppose we'd better be off and deliver Remington to his camp," she said. "We're so grateful to you."

"Maybe we'd better know where this camp is," Kiff's dad said, looking rather helplessly at his wife.

Mrs. Wickers fished another fancy piece of paper out of her bag. It was a camp brochure with a horse's head embossed in gold on the front. "This will give you all the information," she said. "Remington..." she scolded, "put down that fishing rod. We're going."

Remington carelessly tossed the rod on a bench. He gave Kiff a bored look and swept out the door after his parents. The screen door slammed after them.

Kiff's dad stood up with a sigh. "I'll come over to the mainland with you," he told Kiff. "I know you've got your horses at the landing. Go have a good ride, and I'll pick you up at five."

"Thanks, Dad." Despite all the work and responsibility he had at Camp Kokatow, Kiff's parents suddenly looked awfully good to him. He and his dad followed the Wickers down the log steps to the lake. "You're sure there's no chance I'll get stuck with Remington again this summer?"

"I think Camp Saddlemore will have that honour," Kiff's dad grinned. "As your grandmother used to say, Kiff, it takes all kinds of people to make a world."

That's a stupid saying, Kiff thought. The world would get along just fine without people like the Wickers. What his dad really meant was — you couldn't run a business like a fishing camp without wealthy people like Remington and his parents. Too bad.

Over at the landing, the goodbyes were brief. Kiff, Josie and Odie watched the shiny horse van bounce out of sight. "So, did you see the famous Efstur?" Kiff asked.

"I hate to disappoint you, but he looked great," Josie sighed. "Like they said — the best that money could buy. We could only see his head, but he looked really calm and intelligent."

"He's got a white blaze on his face and his ears are fuzzy inside, like a stuffed bear," Odie added.

"And his forelock falls right over his eyes," Josie went on. "It sort of shimmers when he shakes his head."

"The horse is probably as stuck up as Remington," Kiff laughed. "Imagine having a name that means 'The Best.' I'll bet his dainty little feet would trip all over the trail if we took him out with our horses!" He stroked Smoke's grey nose fondly.

Kiff was sure that if he struck it rich in a gold mine, he wouldn't turn into a loser like Remington. That reminded him of something. He reached into Smoke's saddle bag for his gold rock. He needed to get back to the Carter Mine. There was more where that came from!

4

Remington the Raccoon

When Remington Wickers opened his eyes, he
thought at first he was at Camp Kokatow. There
was the same old-wood smell surrounding him,
the same sound of lake water slapping the shore.
Then, all of a sudden, a horse whinnied, right
outside his window! WUNHA-WUNHA-WUH.

Remington grabbed his pillow to his ears and
groaned. Now he remembered the Camp
Saddlemore sign swinging over the gate when
they arrived last night. He remembered his parents dumping the horse van and all his stuff at
this dinky log bunkhouse. He remembered them
driving off and leaving him. He was at horse
camp!

He poked his head out from under the pillow.
The other three campers in his bunkhouse were
just lumps in their bunks. It must be early. Rem-

ington sat up and stuck his head out the open window beside his bed. There were horses out there, all right. The whole place smelled like a barn.

There was a sudden commotion outside the bunkhouse door. The door banged open. A teenager pushed his grinning face inside for a second and pounded on a pot with a big metal spoon. "All right, you Raccoons, rise and shine. Breakfast in ten. Be there."

The other three "Raccoons" shot up in bed as if they were on wires. They got up and fumbled into their clothes and dashed for the door without even looking at Remington. They all knew each other, he'd found out last night. They had all been to Camp Saddlemore last year.

"Hey!" he shouted, as the last one pounded down the bunkhouse steps. "How did we get to be Raccoons?" No one stopped to answer.

Drips! Remington thought. You won't catch me rushing around just because some teenager bangs on a pot. He put on his riding clothes and strolled out into the bright sunlight. Paths of red sand led through the trees to the other bunkhouses. A wider path led to the lakeshore and a beach. Behind the bunkhouses was an open space with a riding ring and a large main building, made of logs. That must be where they served breakfast, Remington thought. He was starting to feel hungry.

But there was no breakfast left. On a long table, where the food had been set out, there were a few prunes, a big bowl of cold oatmeal, and a pitcher of powdered orange drink. He couldn't eat any of this disgusting gorp. And he only drank freshly-squeezed orange juice.

Remington stood there for a while, watching the other campers noisily gulping down bacon and eggs and waffles. Then he headed for the door. He'd find somewhere else to have breakfast.

"Sit down!" Someone grabbed him by the sleeve. "The camp director's speaking!" Astonished, Remington squeezed in between two other kids at the table.

"Good morning, campers," a large lady at the front was saying. "As you all know, my name is Melba Mountjoy. There are just one or two things we need to say about today's program, before you get out to your horses."

"She'll talk for twenty minutes," Remington heard one of the campers giggle.

Half an hour later, Mrs. Mountjoy was still telling them how, before she was married, she had been a Carter, how her grandfather had discovered gold on this very spot, and how the Carter Mine had made the whole family very rich.

"But the wilderness was in the blood," Mrs. Mountjoy droned on, "and I could never rest content until I returned, with my husband, and created this camp for young equestrians on the very spot where my grandfather made his fortune."

The campers had heard all this before. They coughed and scuffled their feet. Mrs. Mountjoy's voice rose to cover the babble as she described the camp routine.

"...and each afternoon we have a rest period, during which campers must stay *in* their bunk-houses; followed by another two-hour session with the horses..."

Remington listened in shock. Not only did you have to race for food three times a day, but between meals, every second was planned. There was not one hour when you could do what you wanted. No time for TV or video games. In fact, he hadn't even seen a TV since he'd arrived!

How had he let his parents talk him into this? He wanted a horse, not a prison sentence. Just wait till they heard about this place. He shoved back his chair to stand up.

"Sit down!" someone hissed. "You can't move until she stops talking."

Remington couldn't believe it. This camp was definitely a mistake.

It got worse outside, with the riding instructor. Everything was rules, rules, rules. Walk this way, stand this way, hold your elbows this way. Even the horses had to walk in a certain direction in the riding ring. Maybe he didn't need a riding camp, after all. Maybe his parents could get him a private trainer.

"I think I'll just be going," he said to no one in particular. If he hurried, he could get in touch with his parents before they left on their Eco-cruise. He headed for the path that led to his bunkhouse.

"Just where do you think you're marching off to?" The same teenager who had banged the pots grabbed Remington's arm. He had big teeth and brown curly hair.

"Back to my bunkhouse." Remington tried to shake off the teenager's grip.

"Oh, no, you're not. All the campers have to saddle up now for the morning ride."

"But I don't want to saddle up." Remington shook his arm again. "I just want to go back to my bunkhouse."

"Not a chance," the teenager grinned. "You're that kid from St. Catharines with the Icelandic horse, aren't you? Well, I'm your counsellor. You're one of my 'Raccoons' and you're coming with me!" His grip was firm, and before Remington knew what was happening, he was inside the riding ring. The counsellor was hustling him towards a small chestnut horse with a blond mane and tail. He had short, sturdy legs and lots of hair over his eyes.

"What happened to Efstur?" Remington was astonished. "He shrank! Why is he so much shorter than all the other horses?"

"Because he's an Icelandic horse. Didn't you know that?"

"But he's the shortest horse here." Remington was shattered. Next to the tall Arabians and standard-breds, Efstur looked like a pony!

The counsellor shrugged. "So? You're no giant, either. He's big enough for you to ride."

I'm going to look ridiculous, Remington thought. "How could my parents be so dumb?" he stormed. "They bought me a midget horse!"

Just then, Efstur shook his head, hard. He glared at Remington from under his shimmering topknot of hair. The counsellor laughed. "You'd better stop insulting him. Don't forget, you have to learn to ride this horse."

"Don't worry," Remington glared at the counsellor. "I'm going to win lots of gold medals and trophies for riding."

"Is that right?" The counsellor laughed again.

"Yes, that's right!" Remington was outraged. "At home, we have a whole room full of my trophies and ribbons. I always win."

5

Berries and Gold

Odie's farm was horse-headquarters for Kiff and Josie. The farm was on the mainland, just outside the town and across the lake from Big Pickle Island and Camp Kokatow. Kiff's island was too steep and rocky for a horse. As for Josie, she lived on Little Pickle Island, which was smaller and even rockier. But Odie's farm was perfect for horses. The fields sloped gently up from the lakeshore. There was plenty of fenced pasture and an old barn that Odie's grandfather had built when he came from Sweden, fifty years before.

Every summer afternoon Josie and Kiff would zoom across the lake in Josie's fast boat, the *Green Hornet*. They would meet Odie and his grandfather in the cool dim barn for chores.

Odie's grandfather, Olaf Pedersen, loved horses. He was the one who had taught them all how to ride, and how to feed and groom their horses. He was excited to hear about Remington's Icelandic horse.

"He may look small," he told them, "but he can carry a 300-pound man. We had horses like that back in Sweden. They were the best." His face lit up with the happy memory.

"The best," Kiff laughed. "That's what Remington kept telling us. I wonder how the little wimp is getting along at that snooty horse camp. It sure wouldn't be the place for us, eh Smoke?" Smoke stood quietly while he brushed her smooth warm flank.

"It might be fun to learn to ride properly..." Josie was cleaning out Skydive's hoof with a hook. He was always picking up stones on the trail.

"What do you call the way we ride!" Kiff said indignantly.

"Oh, we just trail-ride — for fun." Josie finished one of Skydive's feet and picked up another. "Remington's going to learn show-riding and jumping and all that stuff. Don't be such a know-it-all, Kiff Kokatow. Just because you never heard of it, doesn't mean it isn't any good."

"Well, if it means wearing that crazy outfit Remington had on, it's not for me," Kiff said. "He looked like a ringmaster in a circus!"

"Remington was just showing off," Josie said. "He wouldn't wear that stuff all the time."

"I don't know. It said right in the brochure — the kids have to wear *proper* riding gear." Kiff stuck his nose in the air and put on a fake English accent. "Actually, my dear Josephine," he grinned wickedly at Josie, "that outfit might look good on you." Kiff ducked as a clod of dirt flew his way. He picked up a handful of dirty straw to blast Josie back.

"Where are you riding today?" Mr. Pedersen caught Kiff's arm. He didn't like it when they fought.

Kiff put the straw down in a hurry. In this barn, Odie's grandfather was the boss. "I want to go back and look for gold at the Carter Mine," he said quickly. "I got interrupted the other day."

"Forget it, Kokatow!" Josie had a warning expression in her eyes again. "We're going raspberry-picking, as planned. We're not going to waste the whole afternoon collecting useless rocks! My dad says it's the best raspberry summer in twenty years because it's been so dry," Josie added. Her father was Cree, and he had passed on a lot his knowledge about the wilderness to Josie.

"We can do both, up at the mine." Odie stepped in-between them. "Remember, we saw millions of green berries on the edge of the Red Slimes, the last time we were up at the Carter Mine? They must be ripe by now."

Kiff and Josie were still glaring at each other. "I guess so," Josie grunted.

There was nothing she could do. Their parents had made them promise to ride together when they left the Pedersen farm to go exploring.

"If you're going up to the old mine, I want you to promise not to take the horses near the open pit," Odie's grandfather frowned. "In fact, I wish you would keep the horses away from the mine. You never know when there's a nail in an old board, or a sharp piece of metal just under the surface..."

"We'll be careful, Granddad," Odie nodded. "Don't worry."

"It's an evil place, a bad place." Odie's grandfather shook his head. "I remember when the mine first came. They smashed the land around here like an angry fist. Big machines dug up the ground. Dynamite blasted the rock to little bits, just to get the gold! Explosions day and night, till the earth shook..." His eyes were sad with memories.

"That must have been exciting," Kiff's eyes gleamed.

"Sure, but look at the mess they left behind. The open pits and the broken rocks. And those Red Slimes..." The old man shook his head. "I remember when they built the big dam, more than six miles from here. We all wondered what it was for. We found out. They poured so much poisoned muck out of the mine, they needed to build a dam to hold it back." He stared at them.

"Otherwise it might have buried the whole town."

"The slimes are hard now," Josie said. "We can ride on them. Did they used to be wet?"

"Like porridge," Odie's grandfather nodded. "Ground up rock and water mixed up with terrible chemicals. After they got the gold out, they poured what remained on the land like leftover oatmeal."

"The Red Slimes are all dried up, Mr. Pedersen," Kiff tried to cheer him up. "It's like Odie says. Raspberries are growing like crazy, all around the edge."

The old man's face broke into a smile. "That's good. You forget what I said and go enjoy this fine day. Just be careful..." He held Smoke while Kiff swung up into the saddle. Then he patted each horse and waved to the three friends as they filed out of the farmyard.

As usual, Odie rode first, then Kiff and finally Josie. At the edge of the farm, the trail disappeared into a tunnel of birch and poplar trees so thick they met overhead.

"Gold first!" Kiff shouted over his shoulder.

"Berries first!" Josie shouted back.

"GOLD!" Kiff roared. The shouting match continued up the hill, across the main road and down the gravel mining road on the other side. Here the trail changed from soft dirt and moss to sharp stones.

"Will you two shut up!" Odie finally turned to yell at both of them. "All the way up here —

'gold...berries, gold...berries, gold...berries!'"
They had reached the Carter Mine gates — now
just two tumbled pillars of cement and some
rusted wire.

"I can't believe you're not interested in picking raspberries, Kokatow," Josie said. "You're
usually so crazy about free food." The horses
had slowed down to pick their way carefully
over the broken ground.

Suddenly, Kiff slid off his horse, almost causing Josie and Skydive to collide with Smoke.
"Just look at this!" Kiff held up a chunk of rose-
coloured rock that was lying beside the road.
"There could be gold, right here in this rock in
my hand. In fact, there probably is..."

"What makes you think that?" Josie was
scornful.

"Because, this pink rock is the stuff they got
the gold out of, thirty years ago. Very rare."

"You're making this up," Josie said.

"No, I'm not. Why do you think the slimes up
here are red? Because they were made from this
rock, after they got the gold out. I've been read-
ing about it in the *Northern Miner*. It's called red
porphyry, in case you want to know." Kiff
turned the rock over in his hand and then
slipped it into Smoke's saddle bag.

"I don't want to know, and don't keep stop-
ping every time you see a chunk of *por*-what-
ever-it-is," Josie sighed. "The last time we were
up here, you kept hopping off and screaming

about gold and stuffing rocks in your saddle-bags until poor Smoke could hardly move!"

"But what if *you* found a rock with a vein of pure gold? Wouldn't you be just a little bit excited? You'd be rich! You could have anything in the world you wanted."

The other two sat on their horses and looked down at him.

"I don't think gold is all that important," Josie said slowly. "Personally, I'd rather have the lakes and the trees."

"Odie?" Kiff squinted up. "Wouldn't you be jumping up and down and going crazy if you found gold? You could have a Ferrari. A huge fishing boat, like the Wickers!"

Odie gulped. The cowlick in his blond hair stuck up and his face went red, the way it did when he was embarrassed. "I think my grandfather's right." His face got redder. "The gold would be great, but not if you have to wreck everything to get it." He gestured around at the heaps of rock, the rusted fences, the crumbling walls of concrete and the open pit.

"You guys are amazing!" Kiff stared at them in disgust. "This is treasure — right here in the ground." He kicked the rocks at his feet. "Oh, go pick raspberries!"

There was silence for a second. Then Josie said, "C'mon, Odie, we might as well leave him here to sulk..." They turned their horses and rode slowly off in the direction of the Red Slimes.

Kiff climbed back in Smoke's saddle, muttering to himself. "No sense of adventure, that's their problem." He urged Smoke up the Carter Mine hill. As if it mattered if there were a few old pits and some heaps of sand thrown around. There were still thousands of lakes, and forest that stretched clear to James Bay. The old mine looked kind of neat, anyway, like the ruins of a castle. There were huge towers of concrete and down there was the bottomless pit, where you could throw your enemies, like old Moonbrain, the berry-picker!

Down below, Kiff could see Josie and Odie riding along the road to the Red Slimes. He could just catch a glimpse of the bright red sand, vivid against the surrounding forest. The slimes were as wide as a small lake at their widest point and stretched from here all the way to the dam at the far end, the one Odie's granddad talked about. Odie's grandfather hated the Red Slimes, but they made a great place to ride, now that they had dried up. On windy days, the red sand blew high in the air, and you could pretend you were riding your fiery Arabian horse across an endless desert.

And somewhere around here, Kiff was sure, was more gold. Just because the Carters had mined out their vein, didn't mean there wasn't another vein, close by. Maybe down there...in the thick woods on the other side of the hill. Kiff tied Smoke to a poplar sapling and started down the hill, slipping and stumbling on the loose rock.

At the bottom of the hill, he stomped over a rusted wire fence and pushed on through the tangle of young trees. The ground dipped again, steeply. Kiff reached a place where he had to lower himself carefully over huge slabs of stone, like a giant's playground. He was glad he hadn't brought Smoke. A horse could break its leg easily if it slipped through a gap between the rocks. For that matter, a kid could break his leg.

He had to sit down, hang onto tree roots, and inch down the side of a slab three times as high as his head. Under it was a dark space, with an opening big enough to crawl through.

Kiff poked his head inside. The stink of a wild animal's den made him wrinkle his nose. He could feel dry leaves on the floor. Maybe a bear's bed. Kiff was glad there was no bear inside, taking a nap. He got down on his hands and knees and wriggled inside. Then he stood up and waited for his eyes to adjust to the dim light. The cave didn't go back very far, but it was high. A small shaft of sunlight poked through a hole near the back wall. As he looked up, Kiff saw something that made him catch his breath. Ribs of pure white quartz ran across the roof. They glowed against the black rock of the cave ceiling.

Sometimes, Kiff knew, you found streaks of gold in quartz veins like that. He stretched up as high as he could, but his fingers didn't even brush the ceiling. The quartz gleamed out of reach. He backed out of the cave. "Have to get a sample..." he muttered. He plunged into the forest, looking for a rock, a forked branch — anything to help him reach the seams of white rock.

But a few metres from the cave, Kiff made another startling discovery. His feet were wet. He took a few more steps and the water rose to the tops of his riding boots. How could the forest be soaked, when it hadn't rained for weeks, when it was the driest summer in twenty years, according to Josie's father?

Then he noticed the stumps. Scattered through the forest were pale-green poplar stumps with their tops sharpened like stakes. Around each stump was a mound of white wood chips. Kiff picked one up and sniffed it. It smelled fresh and damp. There were grooves on one side, like long tooth marks. These trees hadn't been cut down, they'd been chewed.

"Beavers!" Kiff exclaimed out loud. No wonder the bear, or whatever had lived in the cave, had moved out. The beavers were flooding this land. Somewhere down below, they must have a dam. If I'm going to explore that cave, Kiff thought, I'd better do it before it's under water! As he squished his way back to the cave, Kiff was making a mental list of things he needed right away. Rubber boots, flashlight, rock hammer, collecting bag, rope...

The others were waiting on the road when he got to the top of the Carter Mine hill. He swung up on Smoke's back and rode down to them.

"Find anything?" Josie asked.

"Nope. Just a bunch of stumps and a swamp," Kiff shrugged. "Our furry friends with the big front teeth are making a lake over there on the other side of the hill!" He wasn't going to tell Josie, or Odie, the traitor, anything about the cave. If Odie would rather find raspberries than gold, then Odie was welcome to them!

6

Invitation to Adventure

The trouble with having a secret was that you had to keep sneaking around. For the next week, Kiff nearly went crazy, trying to think of a good excuse to ride up to the Carter Mine again. He was anxious to get back to his cave, chip off a sample from the ceiling and test it for gold. He was even more anxious to find the beaver dam that was flooding the whole area. But he had to do all that without making Josie and Odie suspicious.

Help came from a strange direction — an engraved invitation from Remington Wickers.

"Look at this!" Kiff came dashing into the barn on Thursday afternoon waving a large envelope with a horse's head on it. Josie took a stiff card out of the envelope and read it out loud.

CAMP SADDLEMORE
HOME OF WILDERNESS RIDING ADVENTURES
is pleased to invite
The Kokatow Family
to a display of
EQUITATION
Sunday, July 24th, 2 p.m.
At our Equestrian Centre
R.S.V.P. (Regrets only)

The invitation had arrived at Camp Kokatow that morning. The riding camp was in the same direction as the Carter Mine and his cave. Kiff was hopping up and down with excitement.

"What does 'R.S.V.P., (Regrets only)' mean?" Odie asked, looking over Josie's shoulder at the fancy printing.

"We have to tell them if we *can't* go," Kiff replied. "My parents think somebody should show up. I guess they feel sorry for old Remington with his parents off in the Rain Forest. All the other kids will have somebody there."

"It says, 'The Kokatow Family,'" Josie stroked the raised letters of the invitation. "Aren't your parents going?"

"Can't," Kiff said. "We've got fourteen people arriving on Sunday. Got to give them the big Camp Kokatow welcome." He paused. "So do you want to go — on our horses?"

"Isn't it kind of far?" Odie raised his eyebrows. "Remington told us it was twenty-five kilometres from here."

"Not if we take a shortcut on bush roads." Kiff whipped a battered green map from his back pocket. "Look here!"

He unfolded the map on the barn floor. "See this dotted line? It's a bush road. It cuts across below the Carter Mine to the edge of the Red Slimes. Then you follow the slimes to that old dam your granddad told us about. It must be right near Camp Saddlemore. I figure it's only about ten kilometres if we go this way." He looked up in triumph.

Josie glanced at Odie. "Ten kilometres — that's only an hour's ride for our horses. And it might be fun to see some show jumping and dressage..."

"*Dressage*? Is that where Remington dresses up in those funny pants and that wussy little helmet?" Kiff laughed.

Josie threw him a look of total disgust. "You'd never be able to do it, Kokatow. A good dressage-rider has to be intelligent!"

Kiff ignored her. "Well, Odie, do you think your granddad will think it's okay?"

"He might," Odie said slowly. "If we promise to stick together."

"Of course we'll be together," Kiff shot back. "All the way to Remington's fancy horse camp." But either on the way there, or on the way back, Kiff thought, he might have a chance to slip off on a side trip. At the very least, he'd be able to check out the beaver dam. It must be somewhere right near the trail.

All of the adults had given permission for the ride, as long as Kiff, Odie and Josie promised to start for home as soon as Remington's riding display was over.

"As if we'd hang around a place like that," Kiff laughed.

Sunday morning was bright and clear. Their short cut led them around the bottom of the Carter Mine hill, with the mine ruins towering above them. Then the trail cut through thick forest towards the edge of the Red Slimes.

It wasn't long before Kiff found signs that the beavers were still at work. Chewed stumps were everywhere. The road disappeared into a swamp. Drowned and dying trees leaned crazily in all directions. Staying on the trail was soon impossible, and the horses shied back nervously as their hooves sunk in the black mud.

"I don't understand," Josie said. "It didn't show any swamp on the map. There's supposed to be a little stream called Licking Creek running under the road, somewhere around here."

"Where's your woodcraft, Josie Moon?" Kiff mocked. "Licking Creek has been turned into Slurping Swamp by our little buddies with the big teeth."

"Beavers," Odie agreed. He slipped off Dinah's back and picked up a branch from the ground. "You can see the teeth marks." He handed it up to Josie. "It's still wet. They must have chewed it off this morning."

"We might as well walk the horses." Kiff slid off Smoke's back, and Josie joined him. They dragged the three horses along the edge of the swamp. In the distance they could see the beaver dam stretched across the end of a pond.

Kiff shook his head. "I don't know how you two can complain about the mess the gold mine made. Look what these eager beavers are doing! Flooding roads, making this huge ugly swamp... Ugh! *This place* is an eyesore!"

He urged Smoke forward. "Come on. We'll have to go around the pond and cross the creek below the dam."

It was hard work making their way through the tangle of fallen branches and swampy ground. The horses' feet sank in the mud. Mosquitoes rose up in clouds around their heads. As they got closer to the dam, they found fresh signs of beavers at work. Odie pointed to a clearly marked canal running out through the drowned grass and weeds. "Hey, look! That's where they dragged the trees to the water."

Kiff was not impressed. "Why do they do it?" he groaned, swatting mosquitoes off his forehead. "Why can't they just live in a hole in the ground like sensible animals, instead of doing all this hard work?"

Josie's eyes had been scanning the smooth expanse of pond water. "Hush up, Kokatow," she suddenly hissed. "Look!"

The beaver swam with just his slick brown head out of water. In his mouth was a poplar branch, with fresh leaves still attached. He swam powerfully, making a "V" in the water behind him.

Skydive whickered. At that instant the beaver gave a mighty SLAP with his tail, and dove, branch and all.

"Neat!" Odie said. "They must be working on their dam." Now they could see the dam clearly. It was made of large branches, small sticks and pond mud. It curved around the end of the pond, a hundred metres across. Below it, the water of Licking Creek was just a pitiful trickle.

No wonder they've flooded right back to the cave, Kiff thought. This is a beaver mega-project! He peeled off his riding boots. "C'mon, Odie, let's see if it's strong enough to hold our weight!"

"Kiff, stop! The beavers will think something is attacking their dam," Josie started to say.

Kiff ignored her. He grabbed a stick and used it to balance himself as he stepped out on the dam. It was slippery and full of holes and spaces where the branches didn't meet.

Kiff teetered. One foot broke through, and he sank to his knee. "Hey, Odie," he called. "I'll bet you can't knock me off this thing."

Odie handed his reins to Josie and found a long stick of his own.

"How could he knock you off it, when you're stuck in it!" Josie said in disgust.

"Keep out of this," Kiff shouted, yanking his leg out from between the sticks. His jeans were covered with muck and slime. He had a wicked look in his eye. He charged at Odie who held up his stick to deflect the blow. The sticks snapped in two. Kiff went flying head over heels, into the beaver pond.

"May the leeches eat you alive," Josie said calmly.

"C'mon, Odie, give me a hand and get me out of here," Kiff begged, reaching up the sloping side of the dam. Odie knelt down and held out his hand. Kiff grabbed it, and at the same moment, threw himself backwards. Odie sailed over his head and landed with a splash!

"Got you," Kiff shouted with laughter. "Come on, Moonbrain. Help us both out." He reached out to Josie.

"You've got to be dreaming." Josie shook her head. "In case you two idiots have forgotten, we're supposed to be at Remington's camp in less than an hour."

Odie had emerged, with pond weed draped around his shoulders. They dragged themselves out of the beaver pond and tried to wring out their soggy mud-soaked clothes as well as they could.

"I guess we're not going to make a very good impression at Camp Saddlemore!" Kiff was snorting with laughter.

Josie covered her eyes. "I'll just pretend I've never seen you two before in my life!" she groaned.

7

Remington Shows Off

"Wow, look at that," Kiff said staring. They had ridden to the top of the slimes dam. Under the huge mound of red earth was a criss-cross of cedar timbers, built many years ago to hold back the slimes. Far below them, Odie, Kiff and Josie could see the whole layout of Camp Saddlemore, spread out along the shore of the lake.

Down by the water in a grove of trees were the bunkhouses and the large dining hall. The barns and riding rings were right below them, separated from the slimes dam only by a narrow band of pines.

"Funny place for a riding camp," Josie said. "I wonder if they know the slimes are so near?"

"Probably wouldn't care if they did," Kiff laughed. "Looks like all they do is ride around in those little rings."

In one ring a horse was soaring over a series of fences. In another, several horses were trotting in a neat circle.

"TROT, PLEASE. ALL TROT," came a voice over a loudspeaker. The riders, all in helmets and red jackets, began bumping up and down in a smooth rhythm.

"That's the Command Class," Josie said, pointing to the circling horses. "Now we'll see some *real* riding."

"Sure, Ms. Know-it-all. So where's Remington and his world-famous horse, Efstur?" Kiff shielded his eyes and peered at the riders.

Just then, a voice came booming over the loudspeaker. "GET THAT HORSE BACK. HE'S FOLLOWING TOO CLOSE. GET...BACK!!"

A little chestnut horse was trying to get ahead of the horse in front of him. His blond mane seemed to dance and shimmer above his neck as he trotted along with his nose almost touching the tail of the horse in front. "GET BACK, NUMBER FORTY-THREE." The loudspeaker boomed again.

In the next second, the horse ahead of number forty-three lashed out with his back legs, then shot forward in a sudden burst of speed. His rider fell off. Meanwhile, the little horse who had started it all was running the wrong way around the ring, scattering the neat pattern of horses and riders in all directions. In what seemed like only a moment, the tidy ring of circling horses was a confused mass of rising dust and pounding feet. Kiff, Odie and Josie caught a glimpse of a shimmering topknot through the dust.

"That must be Efstur," Odie cried.

"And poor Remington is number forty-three," Josie exclaimed.

On Efstur's back, Remington was flopping like a rag doll. His feet had come out of the stirrups. He had lost both reins and was clinging to Efstur's mane for dear life.

"STOP, EFSTUR. EF, STOP. HELP, I'M GOING TO FALL, HELLLP!"

"Our boy's in trouble," Kiff shouted gleefully. "Let's go!" He kicked Smoke into a canter and raced down the slope of red sand with Josie and Odie right behind him. They dashed through the thin fringe of pines and up to the show ring.

All of the other horses, excited by Efstur's mad dash, were now galloping crazily, this way and that. Over it all came the screech of the loudspeaker.

"MR. WICKERS, WILL YOU PLEASE GET CONTROL OF YOUR HORSE." Whoever was on the microphone was now screaming at the top of his lungs.

"He's going to get hurt," Josie cried. "He's terrified." She threw herself off Skydive's back and looped his reins around the rail fence surrounding the ring.

"REMINGTON," she shouted, "grab his reins — pull hard!" But Remington was beyond hearing. And even if he could have reached the free-flying reins, Efstur was beyond paying attention to the boy on his back. As the horse swung wildly around a corner, Remington sailed off in the other direction and landed hard in the middle of a cloud of dust.

Josie acted quickly. She threw herself through the rails of the fence, through the haze of dust and blur of trampling feet, and helped Remington up. Tears of frustration were pouring down Remington's dusty cheeks. His helmet had slid to one side and his blond hair was plastered to his sweaty white forehead. Otherwise, he didn't seem to be injured.

"Catch that horse!" he screamed, but there was no need to catch Efstur. He had stopped when Remington fell off and now stood calmly in the middle of all the confusion.

"I hate that stupid, stupid horse!" Remington raised his hand to hit Efstur on the nose.

Josie grabbed his arm. "Remington, stop that! It's not the horse's fault. Come on. Let's get out of here, before we get trampled." She gathered up Efstur's reins and led him towards the side of the ring. Remington stumbled after her.

"Nice riding, Remington," Kiff nodded, as they reached the fence.

Remington glared at Kiff. "It's not my fault," he yelled. "This stupid horse won't do anything I tell him!"

Ef shook his head and neighed softly, as if to add his two cents.

Just then a chubby man in a dusty tweed jacket, top hat and riding boots came hustling over. His face was so red it looked as though his eyeballs were boiling.

"Mr. Wickers!" The kids recognized the haughty accent from the loudspeaker. "Look what you have done, you...you ..." He spluttered to a halt, noticing the three of them and their horses for the first time.

"And who, may I ask, are you?" He sniffed, as if inhaling the odour of pond scum. His eyes swept Kiff's and Odie's grimy jeans and mud-streaked faces. Suddenly those furious eyes swung back to Kiff's grubby Camp Kokatow T-shirt as though he would bore holes through the cotton.

"CAMP KOKATOW," he hissed. "Isn't that...aren't you?"

"We're Remington's...uh, friends."

"You signed the papers!" the large man said, breathing out the words with an enormous gust of relief. "And where — " his eyes swept around them, "— are your mother and father this afternoon?"

"Oh, they didn't come," Kiff said, breezily. "We just rode on over ourselves to watch Remington ride. Quite a show you put on here." The corners of Kiff's mouth twitched.

"They...didn't...come? They're...not *here*!" The man's voice was rising, and his face was glowing red again. "I *see*." The chubby man gripped Kiff's shoulder. "How can I reach your parents? I really must get in touch with them as soon as possible."

"Well, you could send a message back with us," Kiff hesitated. "We rode over, like I said…"

"Don't you have a phone at this…this camp?" the man blustered. "I'd like to reach them immediately." He glared at Remington.

"Well, we do have a radiophone on the island," Kiff said. "But it's for business, not personal calls. It's awfully expensive."

The man wiped his perspiring brow. "We'll go and phone them right now."

"I don't know," said Kiff. "Last year I got in major trouble for giving the number to all my friends. You see, we pay the long distance charges and…"

"Never mind all that! Just come this way. I'll pay. Just give me the number." He steered Kiff away.

Kiff hated being steered. "Well, I'm not sure anyone will be there, on a Sunday. It's a fishing camp, see. We all go fishing…" He might as well have been talking to the engine of a freight train. The fat man, huffing and puffing, went shunting off, with Kiff in tow.

"Who was that?" Odie's eyes were round.

"That's Mr. Mountjoy," Remington said, miserably. "He's the camp director. He wants to throw me out."

"He can't do that!" Josie was outraged.

"He's been faxing complaints about me to my parents in the Rain Forest every day," Remington said. "But they never fax back." He stared at them with his pale blue eyes. "He wrote to Camp Kokatow, too. I suppose I'll have to go there, until my parents get back."

8

Get Me Out of Here!

"Come on, Remington, the camp doesn't look that bad," Josie said, glancing around. The horses looked terrific — gleaming bays, pintos, tall Arabians with shiny black or white coats. It was a horse-lover's paradise.

"They never let you watch television," Remington screeched. "They make you eat globs of disgusting stuff and clean out horses' dirty stalls. It's horrible! I hate every single, stupid second of this stupid camp!"

"Don't you have any time to just hack around?" Odie asked.

"Round, and round, and round, in a stupid, stupid circle!" Josie thought Remington was going to burst, he was so furious. "That's all we ever do. *Walk, please. Trot, please. Canter, please. Stop, please. Line up, please.* And this stupid *horse*!

He won't do anything he's told!" Remington gave a vicious tug at the reins, and Efstur gave an angry snort.

Josie didn't think it would help, right at this particular moment, to tell Remington that it wasn't Efstur's fault. In fact, she felt more sorry for the little horse than she did for Remington. How confused and frustrated Ef must be, being ridden so badly every day, round and round in a ring.

"Don't you ever get to go for a trail ride, or just canter across a field?" she asked.

"We have to pass all this stuff in here, first." Remington waved at the hated ring. "I'll never pass. I'll be riding around and around forever!"

Odie patted his shoulder. Remington flicked his eyes over to where Odie's hand had left a dirty smudge on the scarlet jacket and brushed it fiercely with his hand. "Look what you've done. We're supposed to keep clean!" Suddenly Remington stared at Odie. "Ugh! Look at you. What happened to your clothes?"

Odie shrugged and grinned. "We had a little accident in a beaver pond," he explained. "Hey, here comes Kiff."

Kiff was running. His eyes were as round as marbles. "This place is barbaric!" he panted. "Do you know what they make him do? They make him eat *prunes*! I saw them in the dining hall."

Josie burst out laughing. Out of all the awful things happening to Remington, Kiff *would* focus on the prunes.

"What's funny about it — this is no laughing matter, Moon!" Kiff said. "That Mountjoy is a tyrant in a top hat!"

"What did your parents say?" Odie asked.

"Nothing...they weren't home. Out fishing, like I told the man," Kiff said.

"THE NEXT EVENT WILL BE THE TRAIL-RIDING COMPETITION. WILL THE RIDERS PLEASE GET IN POSITION," came the grating voice on the microphone.

"Oh, help," Remington cried. "Efstur is supposed to be in that competition too..." He looked around in desperation. "I've got to get out of here."

It was too late.

"Mr. *Wickers!*" A large woman in a cowboy hat, a tight pair of leather chaps and a fringed vest was barrelling down on them.

"That's Mrs. Mountjoy," Remington had time to whisper, before Mrs. Mountjoy seized Efstur's reins in one hand and Remington's arm in the other.

"You're supposed to be in Western riding gear for this event, Mr. Wickers," she cried. "And where's your horse's western saddle and tack? Oh — come along, I'll help you get changed."

"But he doesn't want to..." Josie started to protest. It was useless. Mrs. Mountjoy towed

Remington and Efstur away at a trot, towards a large barn.

"I hate bossy people like that!" Josie steamed.

"Me too." Kiff grinned at Odie. "Of course, we don't know anyone like that, do we, Odie? Someone who always thinks she knows what other people should be doing...?"

"If you're comparing me to that rhinoceros..." Josie spluttered.

"Come on, you two. Quit it," Odie protested. "What are we going to do about Remington?"

Kiff put one boot on the rail of the show ring and considered. "Well, in one way, old Remington has exactly what he deserves here," he said. "Except for the prunes, I mean. Nobody deserves that!"

Just then, the loudspeaker called once again for the trail-riding event to begin. Equipment for the event had been set up around the ring. All the other horses and riders were lined up outside the entrance.

There was a deep sigh over the loudspeaker. "ALL RIGHT...WE'LL START WITHOUT MR.WICKERS. THE FIRST HORSE WILL BE MISS THOMPSON, PLEASE, ON DYNAMO."

A few riders later, Remington appeared at the entrance, sitting nervously on Efstur.

"Now *that's* a ridiculous outfit!" Kiff burst out laughing.

The Wickers had certainly spent the maximum on riding gear, Josie thought. Poor Efstur was loaded down with more bronze and leather knick-knacks than a circus pony. As for Remington, he looked like a fringe on horseback. Every article of clothing had long, swaying leather fringes.

"REMINGTON WICKERS, ON EFSTUR..." the loudspeaker announced, as he rode into the ring.

Efstur obviously hated that ring. He tossed his mane and started to trot briskly away from the first post. Here, Remington was supposed to lift a yellow raincoat off the post and put it on while still on Efstur's back.

"But he can't even keep his balance up there, let alone put on a coat!" Josie groaned. "I can't look!" Remington was clutching the reins with white knuckles and swaying from side to side as though his huge cowboy hat made him top-heavy. He made a lunge for the yellow coat the next time Ef breezed by the pole and managed to catch it by a sleeve. The pole toppled over and bumped along behind, with the coat still caught on the top.

"STOP, EFSTUR!" Remington screeched. Efstur stopped, right in front of a gate. For the second part of the event, the rider had to open this gate, ride through and latch the gate again, without getting off the horse. Tugging and yanking, Remington managed to rip the coat off the dragging pole and stuff his arms into the sleeves. Efstur danced nervously at all this yellow plastic flapping around on his back.

"STAND STILL!" Remington roared. He leaned forward to grasp the gate latch. At this moment, Efstur suddenly jerked sideways. Before he knew what was happening, Remington was hanging on the gate, and Efstur was galloping around the show ring, joyfully kicking up his heels.

"We've got to do something," Josie said, again. "They aren't teaching Remington anything, and he's going to ruin that horse!"

"MR. WICKERS, WILL YOU KINDLY REMOVE YOUR MOUNT FROM THE RING! NEXT RIDER, PLEASE..." The loudspeaker voice sounded close to a total breakdown.

Remington got down off the gate, with difficulty. He came limping over with the long yellow raincoat trailing to his ankles.

"MR. WICKERS, KINDLY RETURN THE COAT TO THE POST — IT'S PART OF THE COURSE EQUIPMENT," the voice shouted hysterically.

"Well, what do you want me to do first, get my stupid horse out of here or hang up the coat? Make up your stupid mind!" Remington shouted back. He was clearly at the end of his rope, too.

"I'll get Ef out of here — you take the coat back," Josie said. She slid through the rails and went after Efstur. Remington shrugged out of the yellow raincoat, hurled it at the judge and stomped out of the ring. He kept stomping until he was as far from the hated show ring as he could get. Josie managed to grab Efstur and the three followed Remington, leading their horses.

"Well, that does it," Remington glared at them. "They'll throw me out for sure, now."

All three were silent, watching him.

"I never should have come here," Remington said. "It's not what they said in the brochure. This is a torture camp. I'm leaving, and they can keep this stupid horse, too."

"Wait a minute," Kiff said. "Where are you going to go?"

"To your place." Remington's eyes widened. "Your parents signed the paper."

9

Kiff to the Rescue

"That was just if your parents had an emergency," Kiff said. "It didn't say anything about you messing up and getting kicked out of camp."

Remington looked astonished. "But you see what they're like. I can't stay here!"

"Well, it's not that much different at Camp Kokatow," Kiff reminded him. "We don't have prunes every morning, it's true. But you'd have to work hard."

"What kind of stuff?" Remington looked sideways at him from under his cowboy hat.

"Well, there's cleaning the fish house after the fishermen have been scaling and gutting their catch — now that's an awfully smelly job. Then there's washing dishes for forty people, cleaning outhouses, scrubbing floors, piling firewood —

and of course, we'd expect you to help muck out the horses' stalls over at Odie's farm, and feed and water the horses…"

Remington's eyes looked ready to pop. "You have to do all that?"

"Every day," Kiff nodded. "And then there's the extra jobs. Like getting leeches for bait…"

"Bloodsuckers?" Remington's face grew pale.

"Hundreds of them," Kiff nodded again. "Thousands. You put some rotten meat in a pail in a shallow bay, and when you come back, it's just crawling with leeches. We get some dandies — about this long…" Kiff held up his hands.

"Not bloodsuckers! I CAN'T…" Remington started.

"Of course, you can't," Kiff shrugged. "That's why you shouldn't come to Camp Kokatow. You should stay right here where you belong."

"Oh, here you are!" Mr. Mountjoy stormed down on them. He was so angry he was sputtering. "Get your horse unsaddled and brush him down well, Mr. Wickers. Then change your clothes and wait for me in the bunkhouse."

He wheeled on Kiff. "I'm still trying to get hold of your parents," he said. "How long do these *fishing* trips usually last?"

"Oh, until they catch enough fish," Kiff said, casually. "Sometimes, hours and hours. But anyway," he added, "I don't think you have to worry about reaching my parents. I think Mr. Wickers has decided to stay."

Mr. Mountjoy started to huff and puff again. "Well! I'm not sure. I don't know if we can allow him to stay. We've never had such an unco-operative camper. He doesn't do what he's told, he refuses to take instruction, and he's bad-mannered and rude!"

"Stop it!" Josie broke in. "You can't talk about Remington like that when he's standing right there! He's a person, not one of your lumps of porridge."

Remington was looking from Kiff to Mr. Mountjoy and back again, a look of helpless fury on his white face.

"This is none of your business," Mr. Mountjoy spluttered at Josie. "I'll see *you* in your bunk-house in half an hour..." he told Remington sternly and marched away.

Josie's face was bright red. "Kiff...?" she faced him. "We have to do something!"

Kiff had made up his mind. "Relax, Moon-face," he said. "We have half an hour before Mountjoy comes looking for him." He turned to Remington. "Well, what about it? Are you going to come with us or not?"

"You mean...right now?" A gleam came into Remington's eyes. "You mean, get out of here right now?"

"Sure," Kiff said. "Let's ride! Just come the way you are. Odie and I have lots of normal clothes you can wear. Your parents can collect all the rest of this junk, later. What's the matter?"

Remington's chin had sunk down to his chest. He looked like he was going to cry. "I can't ride," he said. "I'm never getting on Efstur's back again."

The three friends stared at him. This was a problem.

"I guess you can ride Smoke," Kiff said finally. "I'll ride Efstur for you, as a special favour." He patted Efstur's fuzzy forelock. "This is going to be fun."

"I don't want to ride Smoke either!" Remington said. "Falling off a horse hurts, in case you didn't know."

"You won't fall off," Kiff promised him. "You'll be in a line with the other horses. Smoke won't run away with you. Come on. Let's get out of here before old Killjoy comes looking for you!" Remington looked anxiously in the direction of the bunkhouses.

"You don't even have to hang onto the reins," Kiff went on. "We'll tie Smoke behind Dinah, and you can hang on to the saddle horn. It's easy. You can do it. Or..." he grinned wickedly, "you can wait for the Mountjoys to decide what to do with you. It could be days before they reach my parents."

"Okay!" Remington said suddenly. "I'll try." But he seemed almost paralysed with fear as Kiff helped him up on Smoke. He gripped the saddle horn with both hands and stared straight ahead with a look of doom on his face.

"Poor Remington," Josie said. "That fall must have really shaken him up!"

They rode up the slope out of camp in single file. First Odie, then Remington on Smoke, then Kiff and Josie.

They retraced their route. First up the sloping slimes dam. Then onto the trail that led around the edge of the Red Slimes. In some places, the fine sand had blown into high dunes, rippled by the wind. The low afternoon sun caught it and made it glow a rosy red.

"What's all that red stuff?" Remington pointed.

"That's the Red Slimes," Kiff explained. "It's sand now, but it used to be gold rock. They ground it into dust, got the gold out, and dumped the rest here."

"That's weird," Remington said. "Although it might look nice in a sandbox."

Josie sighed. "No, you wouldn't want it in a sandbox, Remington. It's full of arsenic and cyanide and deadly stuff like that. They used all those chemicals to get the gold out of the rock dust."

"Speaking of deadly, the Mountjoys will be going crazy looking for Remington, right about now," Kiff chuckled. "They deserve it."

"Are you sure your parents won't mind us bringing him back?" Odie asked Kiff over his shoulder.

"No, I'm not sure," Kiff admitted. "In fact, they'll probably have a fit. But once they meet those two Mountains of Joy back there, they'll see that I had no choice. In the meantime, I'll just have to talk fast."

"How on earth did Mr. and Mrs. Mountjoy end up here?" Josie asked Remington. "They don't seem to be the wilderness type."

"The land belonged to Mrs. Mountjoy's grandfather," Remington explained. "It used to be a gold-mining camp, or something."

"You mean, her grandfather was Mr. Carter!" Kiff cried.

"Yeah. They all got rich from the mine and moved to New York."

"Mr. Carter's *granddaughter*!" Kiff said. "It's unbelievable." It wasn't nice to think that's what might happen to your grandchildren if you got filthy rich.

"But why would anyone come away up here to start a riding camp?" Josie shook her head. "Why not stay in New York and ride?"

"Everybody wants to go somewhere weird and far away," Remington said. "Like my parents, rushing off to the Rain Forest. They're probably eating roasted toads or something, right now."

"Well, this isn't the Rain Forest!" Josie said. "And it's not weird and strange, either."

"It is if you're from St. Catharines," Remington sighed. "All these Red Slimes, and stuff."

They rode in silence for a while. Kiff was astonished to see how brave and sure-footed Efstur was. The little horse seemed to dance over the rough spots in the trail. "Must feel good not to be going in circles, eh, boy?" he said softly, reaching forward to pat Efstur's neck.

"Enjoying the ride?" he called ahead to Remington.

"NO," Remington snorted. "Once I get off Smoke, I'm never getting on another horse as long as I live!" He leaned low over Smoke's neck and sneezed. "I'm probably allergic to horses, anyway," he sniffed. "I'm allergic to hundreds of things."

As they slogged past the beaver dam, Kiff thought it looked a little higher, and wider. He pictured the pond, flooding further and further back into the woods — right up to his cave. Tomorrow he'd get back there and check. Maybe he could ride Ef. The Icelandic horse didn't seem to hate the slimy, sucking mud along the edge of the pond, the way the other horses did.

"Maybe it won't be so bad having old Remington, if I can ride you once in a while," Kiff chuckled, ruffling Efstur's mane.

Half an hour later, he slid off Efstur's back in the pasture of Odie's farm. "Here we are," he told Remington.

"*This* is Odie Pedersen's farm?" Remington wrinkled his nose in disbelief. He stared at the old barn and the sheds. "It doesn't look like a farm! It's all falling down and rusted."

"Well, Granddad doesn't do any farming any more," Odie said. "He's retired. He just keeps it because..." Odie faltered.

"Don't apologize!" Kiff said. "It's a great farm, Odie. And Remington, get your nose out of the air. You're going to love this place — or it's back to Camp Saddle*burn*! You got that?"

Remington glared at Kiff. "You can't make me!" he said. "Anyway, I'm not staying here. I'm going to stay at Camp Kokatow — with you."

10

Remington Makes Toast

But at Camp Kokatow, Remington got a real shock. He wasn't the pampered guest anymore.

"You're just one of the family, now," Mrs. Kokatow explained. "You can sleep in the spare bedroom, next to Kiff's."

That was all right. He was glad he didn't have to share with Kiff. Not only was Kiff's room full of rocks, but he slept with those horrible huskies. Remington was sure he was allergic to them, too. But being part of the family meant other stuff. Like not having breakfast until all the guests were fed at the long lodge table. The smell of bacon and eggs made Remington almost faint with hunger.

"Your job is the toast," Kiff explained. "Just take it out of the racks on the woodstove, slather it with butter and stick it in the warming oven. And don't let it burn."

Remington raised his blond eyebrows. How hard could it be to make toast! He watched Kiff lean eight pieces of white bread on the toasting rack. While he waited for it to get brown, he looked around the big camp kitchen, and got hungrier. Kiff's dad was slicing bacon off a huge slab of meat. Remington had never seen bacon that didn't come already sliced in a package. Kiff was breaking dozens of eggs into a bowl as big as a wash basin. Suddenly, both of them looked up, and sniffed.

"Remington! The toast!" Kiff was flying across the room towards him. Remington turned to see eight slices of bread in flames. Smoke was billowing into the air, filling the kitchen.

"It's okay, I've got it..." Remington grabbed a pot from the stove. "OWWW!" he screamed. The handle was hot.

"Not that," Kiff shouted. "That's the coffee..." But it was too late. Remington had splashed the hot pot over the burning toast, and now the whole top of the woodstove was boiling and sputtering with burning coffee. Remington squeezed his burnt hand and glared at the stove top. There were no burners on this stupid thing. The whole stove was red hot! What a stupid way of cooking!

Later, as he filled the garbage bag with soggy lumps of charred bread, he heard Mrs. Kokatow explain that the breakfast would be a bit delayed, and that no one should worry about the terrible smell, or the smoke pouring out of the kitchen.

"Can't you just plug in a coffee-maker?" Remington asked Kiff, who was trying to clean the coffee off the cast-iron surface of the stove.

"No electricity, you dimwit!" Kiff bellowed. "This is the woods, we're on an island! REMEMBER?"

After breakfast, there were dishes to wash. No dishwasher, of course. The pile of dirty dishes seemed to tower over Remington's weary head. After the dishes, he and Kiff filled the firewood boxes for each cabin and hauled ice from the ice house.

"Okay," Kiff told Remington. "Now we just have the boats to do and then, lunch."

"The boats?" Remington croaked. "What do we have to do with the boats?" He was staggering with exhaustion.

"Wash out the ones that didn't go out fishing this morning," Kiff said. "C'mon, grab a pail and a brush."

They walked down to the dock. There, four fishing boats bobbed up and down in the water. They hauled the first one out.

"What's that smell?" Remington asked Kiff, as they attacked it with a scrub brush.

"Like it?" Kiff asked with a grin. "It's 'Eau de Worms.' One of *my* favourites."

"Worms?" Remington stepped back. It was really a sickening smell — worse than dead fish. "I didn't know worms smelled like that."

"Only when they've been dead too long," Kiff said cheerfully. "Some fisherman must have spilled his can of worms, and they just died and rotted in the bottom of the boat. They really start to reek in the hot sun. C'mon. Start scrubbing!"

Remington held his nose with one hand and scrubbed with the other. Two years ago, when he had stayed here with his parents, it was interesting to see how people lived without electricity. Fires and iceboxes and all that. But then he'd had their fishing cruiser, the *Salmon Snatcher*, with its battery-operated appliances. He'd had his TV and his VCR. This was not the same! Remington's head was aching by the time lunch was over.

"Kiff, take some time off," Mrs. Kokatow told him quietly on her way out the door with a stack of clean sheets. "It's been a long morning." She glanced at Remington and shook her head. "But for Pete's sake, take *him* with you."

"All right, Remington," Kiff said, "let's go over to Odie's farm and work with the horses."

At the word *horse,* Remington's whole body seemed to twitch. "You go." He shook his head. "I'm going to take a rest."

"And who's going to groom and exercise Efstur and muck out his stall?" Kiff grinned at Remington who looked exhausted. "Come on, you lazy slug, let's not waste this whole afternoon."

Remington flushed. "I'm not going." How dare Kiff call him lazy, after all the work he had just done! "I don't care if Efstur is caked with mud and starves to death," he declared. "I'm tired, and I'm staying here." He gripped the table with both hands and hunched his shoulders up.

Kiff glared at him dangerously, but Remington just glared back. His face flushed even darker.

"Okay," Kiff shrugged. "Stay here, and I'll go and look after your horse. And then tonight, you can boogie right back to Camp Saddleburn, where you belong."

"I won't," Remington shouted. Kiff would have to cut his hands off before he'd move from this table!

"Oh, yes, you will," Kiff arched his eyebrows. "That was part of the deal — that you look after your horse."

"No deal! I never want to see that stupid horse again!" Now Remington was roaring.

"What's going on in here?" Josie Moon banged through the screen door and stared from one of them to the other. "I could hear you two screeching down at the dock."

"I'm not screeching." Kiff waved a hand at Remington. "He is. I'm just pointing out that if he doesn't keep his end of the bargain, he can't stay here — not that it's any of your business, Your Nosiness."

Josie's dark eyes flashed from one to the other. "Stop calling people names," she told Kiff. "And Remington..."

"But this wimp..." Kiff started to splutter.

"His name is Remington," Josie said.

Remington started to relax his grip on the table. Josie was sticking up for him — the way she had stuck up for him with Mr. Mountjoy. He was starting to like this girl. "You could call me Wickers," he paused. "Sometimes they call me that at school. But I'm not going over to Odie's," he added stubbornly. "I never want to ride a horse again."

"All right, Wickers," Josie sat down beside him. "You don't have to ride."

Remington made an "I-told-you-so" face at Kiff.

"...but you have to come," Josie went on. "Horses are a lot of work. Odie and his grandfather get up early to feed and water them. We all go over to help groom and exercise them. Then they have to be fed and bedded down again at night..."

"As if I didn't know!" Remington interrupted her. "Horses are nothing but work and bother. And then, they bite you and kick you and won't go where you want!" He looked up at Josie. "It's not fair."

"I'll tell you what's not fair," Josie said. "It's not fair for us to do all your work for you. Ef is your responsibility." She shrugged. "So you have to come and look after him. C'mon. I'll let you steer the *Green Hornet*."

"WHAT!" Now Kiff was outraged. "You never let *me* drive your boat!"

"I didn't say he could drive it, I said he could *steer* it," Josie said. "He can sit beside me and hold the wheel when we're out in the lake."

"Okay." Remington suddenly let go of the table and stood up. Not only was Josie Moon a neat girl, but the thought of holding the wheel of the *Green Hornet* as they zoomed across the lake was irresistible. "But I'm not riding Efstur, for anyone!"

11

Kiff Battles Beavers

They found Efstur happily munching grass at Odie's farm. He trotted over to stick his nose through the fence when they arrived.

"Granddad treats him like a visiting prince," Odie grinned.

"You're a lucky boy to have such a beautiful horse," Odie's grandfather beamed at Remington. "He's all ready for another good ride today."

"You can ride him," Remington told Kiff.

"After our chores," Kiff reminded him. "Come on, Wickers. The dirty stalls are waiting for us."

As it turned out, it was a good thing Kiff had Efstur to ride. Smoke was a little lame after their long ride the day before. They left Remington sitting on the pasture fence after the chores were done.

"What a relief to just ride away and leave him," Kiff called up to Odie, as they followed the trail into the bush, away from Odie's farm. "Did you ever hear such a fuss about a little horse manure?"

Kiff was happy to be riding Ef again. The sturdy, sure-footed Efstur would be much better at handling the rough rocks at the mine. But the others had no intention of heading for the old Carter gold mine.

"Want to ride up to the Radar Tower?" Josie called. "We haven't been there in weeks."

"Okay with me," Odie shouted back. Dinah, as usual, was leading the way on the trail up from the farm.

Kiff was riding last. He had to work out a plan to get off by himself and do some serious prospecting at the cave. "Watch this," he whispered to Efstur. "I'm at my best when planning an escape from Josie the Moonster!"

What felt strange was trying to shake loose from Odie. But Odie had his chance, and he blew it, Kiff told himself. He had a powerful feeling that he wanted to keep the cave and its secrets all to himself. He had all his prospecting gear with him. The rope was coiled around his waist under his sweatshirt. It was strong nylon rope, light and not bulky. He had managed to stow his flashlight and rock hammer in the sad-

dle bag while they were saddling up. All he needed now was a plan.

As they climbed the hill, Efstur whinnied and shook his shimmering mane, as if he were impatient at having to stay in line with the other horses. All at once, Kiff knew what he was going to do.

He leaned down over Ef's strong neck. "That's *right!* You've got a reputation for running away. Okay — let's see you run!"

He wheeled Efstur's head around and urged him forward. Ef took off like a shot. He was a dream to ride. When he broke into his special trot, Kiff felt as if he was floating on the wind. In no time, they had crossed the main road out of town and were back on the Carter Mine trail. Kiff stopped on top of the hill to see if anyone was following. The trail was empty behind him. Now for the cave.

To his great delight, Ef plunged down the rocky slope where Smoke had been too timid to go. "Good for you, Ef," Kiff cried. "You're a real explorer's horse!"

But when they came to the place where the rocks marched down like huge steps, it was too steep, even for the little Icelander. Kiff left Ef under a tree. He tied his rope to another tree and let himself carefully down the rock.

At the bottom was the cave entrance. This time, it seemed darker inside and smelled damp and sour. Kiff fumbled in the backpack for his flashlight. He shone it upwards. To his great relief, the ribs of quartz still sparkled in its beam. He hadn't just dreamed the whole thing!

Now he was looking for yellow. Dull yellow — real gold. Kiff's heart was thumping under his ribs. It wasn't only the money. It was the thrill of discovering a treasure, all by himself.

Slowly, he ran the flashlight beam down every streak of quartz, until he was on hands and knees on the cave floor. There! The flashlight beam picked out a greenish-yellow glow. Kiff used his hammer to chip off a chunk, then wriggled out into the sunlight for a better look. Yes! There were large golden flakes all through the white crystal.

Kiff thought he would burst. Eagerly, he scratched at the flakes. Some of the gold stayed under his fingernail. It was soft. It was gold!

He danced up and down on the soggy earth. "I'M RICH!" he screamed into the silent forest.

At that moment, Kiff felt cold water seeping through his boots. He looked down. His boots were black and muddy. His knees had wet patches from kneeling in the cave. The cave floor had been dry before, Kiff remembered. But now it was flooding, just as he had feared. Those brainless beavers!

Kiff took a few more steps away from the cave. It was true. Only a metre or two from the cave entrance, there were freshly-chewed stumps. A slippery wet slide cut through the forest where the beavers had dragged the poplar branches to the open water. Kiff whirled around and dashed back to the cave. He chipped off as much of the quartz rock as he could carry and scrambled back up the rope to Efstur.

"C'mon, boy," he urged. "We have to find a faster way down to the dam." He bent low over the horse's mane as they shoved through the dense forest back to the road. Now they were headed back in the direction of Camp Saddlemore. The beaver pond was just a kilometre or so ahead. Once again, Efstur settled into his smooth, effortless stride, and in no time, they had reached the edge of the black ooze.

As they slogged through the muck to the dam, Kiff could see that the beavers had almost totally blocked the creek. It was hard to find the tiny stream of water that was still trickling through. That would be the weakest spot, Kiff thought. He slid off Efstur's back.

Kiff didn't stop to take off his boots. They would help on the slippery sticks. He attacked the dam as if it were an enemy, clawing at its tangle of sticks and mud, hurling branches away, enlarging the stream. Soon the force of the water helped him out. As it gushed through the opening he had made, it washed away the smaller sticks and weeds.

"Hurrah!" Kiff cried. "I'm doing it...I'm winning!" The stream was now a torrent, rushing and gurgling through the dam, getting larger by the second. Kiff was drenched, but he didn't care. He plunged in his arms and threw the sticks to both sides, until he was up to his waist in water. The sound of the rushing water was so loud, Kiff didn't hear the horses, sploshing through the swamp towards him.

"KOKATOW!" He finally heard Odie's cry. "WHAT DO YOU THINK YOU'RE DOING?" Kiff whirled around to see Odie, panting and red-faced, staring at him in shock. Josie was beside him.

"What does it look like?" Kiff shouted. "I'm wrecking this...beaver dam!" He went back to tearing and stomping and kicking at the dam.

"KIFF! STOP THAT!" Josie Moon had leaped up on the dam and was trying to stuff the sticks back in, as fast as he yanked them out.

"They're flooding the whole blinking universe!" Kiff grabbed Josie and stared into her face. "I'm trying to stop an environmental disaster here!" He was puffing so hard, he could hardly breathe.

"But this dam is their home, their protection!" Josie was jumping up and down in anger. "They must be going crazy over there in the pond. Look what you've done!" She pointed to the wide stream of water flowing out of the dam. Just then, the whole centre of the dam gave way, and water gushed through, carrying branches, sticks and mud with it.

"Yes, I've wrecked it, haven't I?" Kiff stopped and mopped his forehead with a muddy hand. In a few hours the water would be much lower than the cave. His discovery would be safe!

"I knew you were a jerk, but I didn't think you could be cruel to animals!" Josie's eyes flashed. "YOU ARE THE LOWEST OF THE LOW, KOKATOW!"

"And she rhymes, too," Kiff laughed. He glanced up at Odie. Odie wasn't laughing. He was staring at Kiff with that embarrassed look again.

"All right." Kiff climbed out of the stream. He was dripping and muddy. "It's just a beaver dam, for Pete's sake. No big deal."

"It's a big deal to the beavers, moron," Josie stormed. "The only way they can keep safe is to build their lodges in the middle of a deep pond. Once the water is gone, all their enemies can reach them."

"So they'll have to move — start another pond somewhere else," Kiff looked with satisfaction at what he had done. "I just pulled the plug on this one."

12

Remington Gets a Lesson

Back at Odie's farm, Remington watched the horses disappear among the trees. On the other side of the farmyard, Odie's granddad was tossing dirty straw high onto the manure pile. Pew! Remington thought. How can he do that without holding his nose?

He had never met a grown-up like Odie's grandfather. He didn't talk much, for one thing. Odie said his grandfather was from Sweden. Maybe that was why. Or, maybe he was so different because he was old. Remington didn't know any other old people. None lived in his neighbourhood, and he didn't have any grandparents. The only old people he saw were on TV.

Remington wished he had a TV. It was tiring, looking at real life the whole time. He sighed, climbed off the fence and followed Odie's granddad into the dim light of the barn.

"Can I watch TV?" he asked.

Odie's granddad made wheezing noises. Remington finally realized he was laughing.

"So, you're the boy who doesn't want to ride the splendid Icelandic horse," Odie's grandfather smiled at him. "He's a horse from the past, you know. The old god Odin had a horse like that. Name of Sleipner. But he had eight legs."

Remington stared at Odie's grandfather. What was he talking about? Was he crazy, or just deaf? He tried again.

"CAN...I...WATCH...TV?"

"Such a nice day," the old man laughed, "to be sitting in front of the tube."

What was so funny about watching TV? Remington wondered. He let the corners of his mouth droop. "I'm bored," he said. *Bored* and *allergies* were two words that usually got adults moving.

Odie's grandfather started to sweep the floor again with a big push broom. The dust swam in shafts of sunlight that filtered in through old barn boards. "I never got a TV out here. I have one in town, for the winter. I like to watch the hockey games." He stopped sweeping. "But if you're bored, why didn't you go riding?"

"I hate horses," Remington said. "If you like Efstur, you can have him. I don't want him."

"It's a nice offer," Odie's grandfather smiled. "But I'm too old for a lively horse like that! He can run all day and never get tired."

"I know!" Remington exclaimed. "He runs too fast."

"Odie, my grandson, and his friends didn't know much about horses when they first got them." Odie's grandfather leaned on his broom handle. "Did they ever tell you how they got those horses? It's a good story."

"No," Remington said. He sat down on a wooden box. "I thought they bought them." How else did you get anything, he wondered.

"Oh, no...that wasn't the way," Odie's grandfather shook his head. "Let me tell you, not one of their parents would have bought those kids a horse. Not even my own daughter, Odie's mother. You see, Josie lives on that little scrap of an island, and the Kokatows are too busy with their fishing camp..."

"So how did they get them?" By now Remington was curious.

"Well, that Josie Moon — when she found out I used to keep horses here, for farm work, she used to just come over and sit in the empty stalls. She'd run the old harness through her hands and dream." He chuckled. "She was so crazy for a horse!"

Remington nodded. He could picture Josie doing that.

"And that Kokatow boy — he would tease her so bad, I felt sorry for her. Kiff, he's a bit like

Loki. That's the Norse god of mischief." Odie's grandfather shook his head. "And then, one day, by Odin, she *found* a horse!"

Remington's eyes grew larger.

"But I guess you don't want to hear all that story, seeing as how you hate horses..."

"I don't hate hearing about them," Remington said, quickly. "What do you mean, she found a horse?"

"She found more than one! Come over here and look at Smoke. She was one of them." Odie's grandfather opened Smoke's stall and clucked softly to lead her out into the open part of the barn.

"Just hold her there, while I get some stuff to rub on her sore legs."

"But, I ..., no...I..." Before he knew it, Remington was reaching up to hold Smoke's halter. Smoke twitched her head to shake off a fly, and Remington almost jumped out of his shoes. "Hey," he said. "Don't make any sudden moves like that!"

Odie's grandfather came back with the bottle of liniment and bent over Smoke's right foreleg. "Just hold her nice and steady now, while I rub," he said.

"How did they find her?" Remington said. Smoke was blowing on the back of his neck. He hoped she didn't bite!

"Well, there was a forest fire north of here last year. A bad one, started by some bear hunters up around Ramore. And, there was a handful of horses up there, running wild. People figured they must have come from abandoned hobby farms and such. Horses are pretty close to wild animals. It just takes one generation, and they go back to being feral — that's wild horses."

He straightened up and rubbed his back. "Anyway, the fire drove these horses south, to the shore of this lake, and that's where Josie Moon found them. And once she found them, by Odin, she wouldn't let go of the idea of saving them from the fire."

"And Smoke was one of those horses?" Remington asked. In spite of himself, his hand went up to stroke her soft grey nose. "And they called her Smoke because of the fire?"

"That's right!" Odie's grandfather said. "I think she's well enough to go out in the pasture for some sun and fresh air. Come on. I'll show you how to lead her."

"How do you know she's well enough?" Remington asked.

"Well, see, I run my hand down her leg, and I feel for any lumps, or hot spots. Feel here — this leg is a bit sore, yet..." Odie's grandfather guided Remington's hand to a warm spot on Smoke's leg.

"So you *are* a little bit interested. That's good." The old man's eyes twinkled. "Would you like to learn something about horses? Seeing as we have no television to watch?"

"No! I mean, maybe. Just stuff about wild horses...and how to lead them...stuff like that,"

Remington stammered. Having Odie's grandfather talk to him would pass the time until the others came back.

"Then, why don't I show you how we put the bridle on her…" Odie's granddad reached for a bridle on a hook. "We use a nice soft bridle on Smoke." He handed the tangle of leather straps and buckles to Remington.

"Head piece first, poke the ears through, that's right…" Remington found it easy to follow Mr. Pedersen's directions. He stood behind Smoke's head, held the bridle in one hand and slipped the horse's ears through with the other.

"Good!" Odie's grandfather nodded. "Now we use a snaffle bit — it's copper so she can make spit, and hinged in the middle — a nice kind bit." He settled the bit in the back of Smoke's mouth.

"How do you know she won't bite?" Remington looked doubtfully at the way Odie's grandfather was sticking his hand right in the horse's mouth.

"You have to feel for the space where she doesn't have any teeth," Odie's grandfather laughed, "…like this." Remington's fingers went where he guided, and the bit followed.

"Ugh!" Remington shook his head. "I always got someone else to do this for me at camp. But why are we putting a bridle on Smoke if we're just going to turn her out in the pasture?"

"I thought you might like a little ride," Odie's grandfather's eyes twinkled. "It wouldn't hurt

Smoke to walk around a bit, and then you could show those other smart alecks who think they know so much, eh?"

Remington looked up at Smoke's back. It was a long way up there. He had promised himself he'd never ride again, but suddenly he had a picture of Kiff's eyes, laughing at him. Thoughts of revenge filled his mind. Kiff looking shocked at how well he rode. Kiff having to apologize!

"Maybe," he said. "Could we keep it just between us, that I was getting lessons?"

"That's what I had in mind," Odie's grandfather chuckled again. "Here they come now. We'll start again tomorrow, eh?" He quietly slipped the bridle off Smoke and put the halter back on. Tomorrow, Remington thought, as they turned Smoke out to pasture.

Efstur was in the lead, as the three rode up to the barn. Kiff's face was flushed and excited.

"Boy, this horse can go," Kiff slid from Ef's back and tousled his shimmering forelock. "And smooth! Sometimes I felt like I was riding a rocket!"

"That's the *tolt*." Olaf Pedersen's eyes lit up.

"The what?" Kiff looked puzzled.

"It's a special trot that Icelandic horses have. Nice and smooth for the rider — not bouncy at all." The old man patted Efstur with love in his eyes. "Yes, little fellow, you love to run, don't you?"

Remington backed away. Efstur might look great but he knew better! He noticed that Josie and Odie were very quiet. They unsaddled their horses and brushed them down without a word, while Kiff babbled on about what a wonderful ride he had had.

What had happened out there? Remington wondered. Josie marched ahead of them down to the dock as they headed for home.

Kiff started singing at the top of his lungs. The tune was "Found a Peanut." The words, Remington had never heard before.

Found a beaver dam,
Found a beaver dam,
Found a beaver dam today.
Today I found a beaver dam,
Found a beaver dam today.

Smashed a hole in it,
Smashed a hole in it,
Smashed a hole in it today,
O, today, I smashed a hole in it,
Hope those beavers go away.

Kiff sang it all the way to the *Green Hornet*. As she climbed into the boat, Josie looked up with blazing eyes.

"Stop that, or swim." Her voice was like ice pellets.

"Nobody appreciates my singing," Kiff shrugged, but he stopped.

13

Bear Falls

The next morning, Sheila Kokatow came into Kiff's room and shoved a husky dog off his bed so she could sit down. "That Wickers boy!" she said. "He just asked me if we had a jacuzzi. He wants to take a bath before he starts burning the toast!"

"Don't talk to me about Remington, Mom! Yesterday, he just hung around Odie's farm all afternoon and did nothing," Kiff snorted, "while I..." He stopped. Maybe he'd better not tell his mom about the gold yet. "...while I was riding his horse."

"I suppose we'll survive until his parents get back," his mom sighed, "but now I have some idea why Camp Saddlemore sent all those faxes!"

"It's too bad you signed that dumb piece of paper," Kiff groaned. He rolled over and buried his face in his pillow. "I should have left him at horse camp.

"Mom," he suddenly sat up, "are you or Dad going to Bear Falls this week?"

His mother looked puzzled. "Why, is there something you want?"

Kiff was clutching the rock sample he had hidden under his pillow. He needed to get it to the mining office in Bear Falls and find out how much gold was really in it.

"No…" he stammered. "I just thought I'd like to go and…get a break from Remington, you know?"

"I sure do!" Sheila Kokatow stood up. "Your dad's going in for supplies this morning. I'm sure he'd appreciate some help loading boxes." She sighed again. "I guess I can keep an eye on Remington."

At the town dock an hour later, Kiff was mooring the *Queen* when he heard the buzz of Josie's *Green Hornet* coming in. He stretched out a helping hand, but Josie waved him away.

"I can do it myself," she said, eyeing him coldly. "I just want to say, Kiff Kokatow, that I thought you were turning into a decent human being when you rescued Remington from camp. I was wrong. Nobody who is cruel to animals should even call themselves human!"

Kiff gave her his most maddening grin. If Josie wanted to hate him, she could go ahead.

Later, on the way to Bear Falls, he imagined how surprised they would all be when his gold ore proved to be a fabulous find. Moonface would be forced to apologize. Odie would be excited. In fact, Kiff thought, maybe he should tell Odie about the cave. Odie could even help... He walked up the steps to the mining office, with butterflies in his stomach.

He held out his sample to the woman behind the counter. "I'd like to get this tested," he said. "For gold."

"Where did you find it, young man?" The geologist turned Kiff's rock sample over and over in her hand.

Kiff mentally zipped his lip. No prospector ever told where he found something! How dumb did this woman think he was?

The geologist stopped looking at the rock and glanced up at Kiff. "Oh," she said, "I see. It's a secret."

Of course it was a secret. Kiff hated it when adults treated him like a little kid. "Can I check in this office to see which mining claims are already staked?" he asked.

"No. That's down the hall." She pointed. "Are you thinking of staking a claim?"

"That depends on what you tell me is in that rock," Kiff nodded at the sample in her hand. "How long will it take?"

"Two or three weeks."

"So long?" Kiff was shocked. How long did it take to test one little piece of gold ore?

"Sorry," the geologist said. "We have a big backlog of work."

Kiff turned to leave. "Don't you want to leave your name and phone number?" she called after him.

Kiff paused. If he left the phone number of the camp, his mom or dad would probably get the call. "No," he said. "I'll just come back in and pick up the results. My initials are K.K."

"Real secretive." The geologist shook her head. "This must be quite a find. Did you say there was a lot of stuff like this lying around? Maybe you should bring in some more samples."

"Nope," said Kiff. He reached for the door handle. "I didn't say, and I don't think you need any more." He'd heard lots of stories about claim-jumping. As soon as the news got out that somebody had found real gold, everybody tried to find out where, so they could get there first and stake the land. Kiff felt a shiver of excitement. The geologist had been really interested. It must be gold.

He was going to be rich!

14

Kiff's Secret

When he got back that afternoon, he couldn't wait to tell Odie about the gold. He was glad that today, Remington didn't make a fuss about going to Odie's farm.

"I guess the kid knows when he's beat," Kiff grinned at Josie. Remington was racing ahead of them down the lane.

"You talk as if everything was a war!" Josie was still furious with him.

"Well, with Wickers — it is!" Kiff retorted.

They caught up to Remington at the farm gate. "What's that noise?" he demanded. The growl of an engine filled the air. "That's the tractor," Kiff told him.

"A tractor!" Remington looked surprised. "I thought you said Odie's grandfather didn't do any farming."

"He doesn't, but the hay we buy for the horses comes in big bales. You need a tractor to lift them," Josie explained.

In the farmyard, they could see the old red tractor. It had high, narrow wheels and a metal seat. Stuck on the front was a huge roll of hay, almost bigger than the tractor itself.

"I wish he'd get smaller bales," Josie muttered. "Those big round bales are dangerous."

"Hay? Dangerous?" Remington peered from Josie to Kiff. "Are you trying to kid me?"

"Seriously," Kiff nodded. "Last year, one of those round bales fell off a wagon, rolled right down a farmer's lane, across the road, and squashed a neighbour flat. Killed him. But don't worry," he added. "Odie's there to help his granddad. They know what they're doing."

"I still think they're dangerous," Josie tossed her head.

"You're always so *concerned* about everything, Moonbrain," Kiff laughed. "Doesn't it give you a headache?"

"You give me a headache — you couldn't care less about anything," Josie said in disgust.

"I care! Didn't I rescue poor Wickers here from a summer of prune torture?" Kiff protested. "That reminds me, Remington, your tasks await you..." He pointed towards the barn.

In the barn doorway, the tractor was gently letting down the giant roll of hay. As it backed away, two sharp prongs popped out of the round bale, like a fork out of a hot dog. The hay bale rolled forward.

"How is Smoke today?" Kiff shouted up to Odie's grandfather on the high tractor seat.

"Better," Odie's grandfather shouted back. "But she still needs a few more days of peace and quiet before you take her rampaging around the bush again, Kiff Kokatow."

"Fine. I'll ride Efstur. No problem." He smiled sweetly at Josie. "See how kind and considerate I am?" Nothing could spoil his good mood today. He couldn't wait to get Odie alone and tell him about the gold.

"I've got something important to show you," he whispered in Odie's ear as they saddled up. "Wait till we're riding — till we get rid of Josie."

Odie shook his head. "We're going to get in huge trouble if my grandfather finds out we're not sticking together when we ride — like we promised," he said. "I hate to say this, Kiff, but you're acting a bit crazy, lately."

"I've got a reason. You'll see. We've just got to get rid of Josie…"

"Stop whispering," Josie marched out of Skydive's stall, leading her horse. "I have no intention of riding with you. Just stay away from that beaver pond, if you know what's good for you, Kokatow!"

"What pond?" Kiff asked innocently.

A few minutes later, he and Odie watched Josie ride out of sight. "We don't need her," Kiff said. "Listen, Odie, this is really important. Yesterday I found gold — the real thing. A whole vein of it, not just a few flecks in a rock."

"Yeah? So, where is this wonderful stuff?" Odie squinted over at him.

"I discovered a cave — back before we went to Remington's riding camp." The words rushed out of Kiff. "Yesterday, I got a sample from the cave, and this morning, I took it to Bear Falls, to the mining office."

"What did they say?" Odie asked.

"Nothing — I won't know for a couple of weeks. But they looked...really interested." Kiff paused at the doubtful look on Odie's face. "C'mon, Odie, it's real, I'm telling you! The cave is on the other side of the Carter Mine hill. Wait till you see it. It's amazing!"

"Amazing..." Odie echoed, shaking his head. "What's amazing is the way you never give up!"

They left the horses at the top of the hill. Kiff led the way down to the yellow rope he'd left hanging over the cave entrance. "You go first," he told Odie breathlessly. "Wait for me inside the cave." He handed Odie the flashlight.

Odie lowered himself down the rock. There was a long silence. Then Odie's voice came floating up to him. "I can't see anything, Kiff. There's water in here..."

"Water! In the cave?" Kiff shouted. He scuttled down the rope and splashed inside. "See, there..." he pointed, "where that seam of quartz runs down near the ground..." Kiff straightened up in horror. "You can't see anything. The whole thing's flooded!"

Where the cave floor had been damp yesterday, the water was now ankle deep. Kiff's quartz vein disappeared into a black pool. "I don't understand." Kiff lifted a shocked face to Odie. "The water should be lower — not higher. The pond should be half-drained by now. You saw how fast the water was running over the dam!"

"So that's why you broke the dam," was all Odie said.

Half an hour later, Kiff stood in front of the beaver dam. Once again, Licking Creek was just a small leak in a solid wall of sticks.

"I can't believe they built it up again...in one night!" Kiff stared.

"Believe it." Odie tried not to grin. The beavers had not only repaired the gap in their dam, they'd made it higher.

Kiff's face was white. "They can't flood my cave," he said, between clenched teeth. He hurled himself at the dam, kicking and snatching at the tangle of sticks.

There was mocking laughter from nearby. He looked up to see Josie, leading Skydive, laughing her head off. "One man against a whole tribe of beavers," she snorted. "You'd better give up, Kokatow. I don't think you're going to win this battle."

"Oh no? Wait till I get the results from the mining office. Wait till they find out what's under this...beaver pond!" Kiff was still flinging sticks to both sides. "Then they'll be out here with dynamite and bulldozers! You'll see."

"What's he talking about?" Josie threw a startled look at Odie.

Odie just shrugged. "Ask him yourself," he said.

15

Riding Lessons

Meanwhile, Remington was having his first riding lesson with Odie's grandfather. After the others had ridden away, Remington faced Odie's grandfather with his hands on his hips.

"Let's go," he demanded. "I want to learn to ride — better than Kiff. Are you sure you can teach me?"

"I think so," Olaf Pedersen smiled. "But first we have some other things to do."

In the next hour, Remington found himself putting Smoke's saddle on properly, making sure it was balanced over her withers and doing up the cinch just until it was comfortable. Smoke liked the attention, and Remington learned how to feed her carrots, holding his hand flat and steady, and not jerking it back when Smoke's big teeth lifted it gently off his hand.

"Some horses bite, but she's a good one," Odie's grandfather explained. He patted Smoke affectionately.

"This is taking an awfully long time," Remington said. "We practiced all this stuff at camp a hundred times, and l rode her all the way here from Camp Saddlemore."

Odie's grandfather shook his head. "That wasn't really riding. Smoke was in a line with the other horses. She also knew she was on her way home. So, she didn't care much who was on her back. To really ride, you have to take time to know the horse." He smiled at Remington.

"Now Smoke is starting to like you and trust you. Soon you'll both be ready."

Finally Remington led Smoke out into the pasture. She stood quietly while Odie's grandfather fastened a long leather line to her halter.

"Now when I was teaching my grandson and his friends to ride, I used this lunge line to control the horses. That way, they didn't have to steer while they were learning how to sit and how to use their legs."

"At Camp Saddlemore, they just plunked us up there…" Remington looked miserable at the memory. "And stupid old Ef took off."

"He knew you didn't mean business," Olaf Pedersen chuckled. "Horses have small brains. They don't know much. But they know when you mean business. Get up on that saddle now, and I'll show you how to let the horse know you're the boss."

Before he knew it, Remington had one hand on Smoke's withers, one foot in the stirrup and was slinging his right leg over the saddle.

"Never land with a thump," Odie's grandfather said. "Then the horse knows for sure, you're a beginner. And don't squirm and wiggle around. Sit nice and firm and quiet, like you're in a comfortable chair in front of the TV. Then the horse will feel comfortable, too."

"Nice and quiet. Don't wiggle," Remington repeated to himself. "Okay, Smoke, we're watching *Star Trek* and it's really interesting…" Smoke nickered softly and bobbed her head.

"You look fine up there," Odie's grandfather nodded. "Now, we'll get her to walk. Come on Smoke, old girl. Walk on."

I'm riding, Remington thought. And I like it! He would wait, though, until he was really good before he told the others he was taking lessons.

Odie's grandfather helped Remington keep his secret. Odie did wonder, sometimes, why his granddad looked so pleased whenever Remington's name was mentioned. And Kiff was amazed that he was so eager to go to the farm every afternoon.

A week later, Remington was ready to learn to steer Smoke by himself. He had already learned to sit firmly in the saddle and balance without holding on. He could even trot, no hands. Remington could hardly wait for his riding lesson that afternoon. While the others saddled up for

their ride, Remington brushed Smoke's glossy grey hide until it glowed.

"Smoke's going to catch on fire if you keep that up," Kiff laughed.

"I don't see you putting much effort into grooming Efstur!" Josie remarked.

"Oh, but Efstur doesn't need so much grooming as the other horses," Odie's grandfather told them. "After a thousand years of running free in Icelandic pastures, these horses can look after themselves. Look at this..." He led Efstur out of his stall and held up one foot for the kids to see.

"His foot is bigger than Smoke's and tougher too." He pointed to the underside of the hoof. "This foot can walk over volcanic rocks, or up the sides of mountains."

"That's why he's so good around the old mine site," Kiff grinned. "Let's take the horses up for a wild gallop on the Red Slimes. Ef would really love that."

"Slimes don't sound hard enough to gallop on," Remington muttered. "Doesn't sound like much fun, either."

"That shows how much you know about riding!" Kiff said. "Galloping is the best! And the Red Slimes have been dry for years. You should see them in a strong wind — looks just like a desert sandstorm!"

"Before you go," Odie's grandfather interrupted, "help me fork the rest of this old bale of hay into the feeding bins. I want to move a new bale in this afternoon."

"They can go," Remington said quickly. "I'll help."

They all stared at Remington in surprise. "That's nice of you," Josie said. "But there's no reason to do our work."

"Remington!" Kiff said. "Is this you?"

"The boy is just trying to help an old man." Odie's grandfather shooed them out of the barn. "So go, and let him do a good deed."

"Okay, but be careful moving that big bale, Granddad," Odie said.

"I'll be careful, like always," his grandfather grinned. "Now go and have your gallop."

Remington watched the three horses disappear into the trees. He turned eagerly to Odie's grandfather. "Can I ride before we do the hay? Can I steer today?"

Odie's grandfather nodded. "The hay can wait."

A few minutes later, Remington was sitting straight in the saddle, the way he'd been taught.

"I think you're ready," Odie's grandfather said. He undid the lunge line and handed Remington the reins. "Just hold the reins lightly...that's right...hold your hands just above her withers, don't rest them on her mane. Tuck in your elbows, give her a little nudge with your knees."

Remington took a deep breath, trying to remember everything at once. He pressed Smoke's sides and she walked forward slowly.

"Feel the contact with her mouth." Odie's grandfather walked by his side. "When her head goes forward, let your arms go with it. Feel that?"

Remington wasn't sure he was feeling the right thing. It was such a gentle pull. But he tried to let his arms move forward at the right time, and Odie's grandfather nodded his head.

"That's very good. You're going to have hands as soft as silk. Now, when you want her to stop, give her the signal by sitting down firmly in the saddle, and bring your elbows back so you're pulling back on the reins. GENTLY!"

Remington let his hips slide forward and down so he was sitting heavily. He pulled his hands back softly. To his amazement, Smoke stopped.

In the next hour, he learned to steer her left by pulling with his left hand, and right by doing the same with his right hand. It was so easy, he felt like laughing.

"That Kiff, he's going to get some surprise!" Odie's grandfather smiled, as they turned Smoke loose in the pasture. "You're doing very well."

"Can I ride as well as Kiff?"

Odie's grandfather looked at him with his head to one side. "You don't want to be too much like Kiff Kokatow," he said. "That boy can be too full of mischief. He has to go everywhere at a gallop. A good horseman doesn't have to gallop to show off." He shook his head. "You just be yourself, and take it slow."

Remington looked down at the reins in his hands. He felt a smile coming up from inside.

"Maybe soon, when the other kids go riding in the afternoon, you'll go too, eh?" Odie's grandfather said.

"Not yet. I like just riding around here." Remington wanted to be sure he was one hundred percent ready before he surprised them all.

"And now we'd better move that hay," Odie's grandfather sighed. He handed Remington a long, three-pronged pitchfork and pointed at the pile of loose hay on the barn floor. For a few minutes they worked quietly, tossing hay into the feed bins in each stall.

"Okay, that's good." Olaf Pedersen leaned his fork against the barn wall. "I'll get the tractor and move another bale up for tomorrow. You put away Smoke's tack — by yourself now, right?" The old man sounded tired.

Remington heard the tractor start up as he went to the tack room to hang up Smoke's bridle and saddle. Each horse had its own peg in the small room at the end of the barn with its riding tack hung neatly, ready to go. As he reached for the hook, Remington heard the tractor rev, then suddenly stop. He paused, and let his hand fall. Was Odie's granddad done shifting the bale already?

Suddenly, in the silence, he heard Smoke whinny as if in fear. Something was wrong.

Remington flew out of the tack room, along the dim corridor of the barn and out into the blazing sun. He shielded his eyes for a second, then ran.

16

Disaster!

The tractor was tipped on its side. At first, all Remington could see was a huge round doughnut of hay and the wheels of the tractor, still spinning in the air.

"Mr. Pedersen! Where are you?" Remington screamed, still running.

"I'm here." He heard a muffled cry.

Climbing over the top of the ancient tractor, Remington could see where Odie's grandfather had fallen when the tractor flipped. His legs were pinned at an awkward angle under the hay bale. But it was his back he was holding as he moaned.

"The weight of the bale must have tipped us. I jumped...cl...clear," he stuttered between clenched teeth, "so the old tractor didn't g...get me. But my back's twisted, and this blasted bale's on my legs. Don't th...think I can move."

"I'll help get you out," Remington cried, trying to squeeze in between the hay bale and the overturned tractor.

"No! Don't. You might jar the bale loose. She'll r...roll right over me. Just the tractor fork...holding her. You'd better get some help."

"I'll phone 911!" Remington turned to race for the farmhouse.

"Wait!" It was more of a moan than a cry. "No telephone in the old house. No 911 even if there was...hee!" It sounded almost like a laugh.

Remington turned back. This stupid wilderness! No phones. No 911! A person could die out here!

"...ride into town on Smoke. Post Office...or the Fire Hall. Should be someone there." Mr. Pedersen's voice was getting weaker.

"I can't..." All Remington's old fear of riding came rushing back.

"Sure you can, son. Just do...everything I taught you."

Remington felt waves of panic sweeping over him. He felt sick when he looked at Mr. Pedersen's pinched white face. He felt sicker, just thinking of saddling Smoke by himself and riding alone into town. "I CAN'T!" he cried again.

Odie's grandfather stopped moaning. He just lay there with his eyes shut. His face was as grey as his old workshirt. Remington was afraid to leave the old man's side, in case he was dead when he came back. He remembered how Kiff had described the farmer — squashed flat by a rolling bale.

Remington sat very still, with his arms wrapped around his knees. He played over and over in his mind what he should do — get the saddle and bridle from the barn, put them on Smoke, ride Smoke out of the gate and down the lane. He could do it in his head, but he could not make his body move.

Even when he saw the three riders come out of the woods at the end of the pasture, Remington couldn't stand up and shout for help. He couldn't even answer their cries, as they galloped up and threw themselves off their horses.

"Granddad!" Odie shouted. He kneeled on the ground beside his grandfather. "I never should have left," he cried. "I knew he needed me to help with the tractor!"

"Remington, what happened?" Josie's dark eyes drilled into his.

"I didn't see...I think the tractor tipped...The bale was too heavy," Remington said. His own voice sounded slow and fuzzy.

Then there was a short spurt of frenzied activity. Josie dashed off on Skydive to get help in town. Kiff ran for a blanket from the barn and draped it carefully around Odie's grandfather. He and Odie brought boards, and pitchforks, and anything else they could find to prop up the bale and tractor, and relieve some of the crushing pressure on his legs.

After that, it seemed to take a thousand hours for help to come. First the fire truck, then Odie's mother in her van, and finally the doctor, came bumping down the farm lane. As everyone crowded around, Remington knew he was in the way. But it was hard to move; he'd been sitting in one position so long. He finally scrambled to his feet as the volunteer firemen got ready to lift the tractor and bale.

"Remington..." Odie's grandfather let out a cry. Remington came close to hear. "Tell Kiff Kokatow...Smoke needs a few more days rest..." he whispered softly, but his voice was very clear. "Then you show them. Show them what you can do. All right?"

"I can't..." Remington started to say, and then cleared his throat. "I'll try," he said. He stood back, so the doctor could examine the old man. He watched while they rolled him gently onto a stretcher, wrapped him tightly, and carried him to the back of the van. Odie climbed in the front with his mother. The van pulled away, moving carefully over the rutted lane. Remington felt numb — as though he'd been watching too much TV.

"You look wiped, Wickers." Kiff clapped him kindly on the back. "Come on, let's go home."

Remington winced. It was horrible that Kiff was being nice to him.

"Don't look so miserable — there wasn't anything you could do."

If you only knew, Remington thought. I could have gone for help an hour ago. I could have ridden Smoke. Everything Kiff had said about him before was true. He was a wimp, and a loser. And it wasn't true that they called him Wickers at school. His real nickname, that he hated, was "Wickerlips." They called him that, because he used to blubber every time he got hurt in the playground and his lips would wobble. They were starting to wobble now. He bit them to make them stop.

"I can take you in the *Green Hornet*," Josie said.

They closed the barn doors and walked slowly back down the lane to the boat landing.

"It was weird the way Odie knew something was the matter with his granddad." Kiff shook his head. "When we were almost at the slimes, he just suddenly turned around and galloped back down the road, right Josie?"

"Hmmn," Josie agreed. "Something felt wrong to me out there, too. Did you notice something funny about the road, Kiff? The sand was soft, as if it had been raining..."

"Raining!" Kiff snorted. "It hasn't rained in weeks. The woods are so dry they crackle!"

"I know. So how come the road to the slimes was wet?" Josie paused to think. "You don't think the beaver pond could be backed up that far, do you?"

"Who knows?" Kiff shrugged. "Those beavers probably won't quit until they've flooded from here to Hudson Bay!"

"Not that it matters," Josie sighed. "We're going to be too busy looking after the farm to go riding on the slimes. At least until Odie's granddad gets back on his feet."

Remington could feel his lips start to wobble again. "He will get back...on his feet, won't he?" he stammered.

Kiff put his arm across Remington's shoulders. "Sure he will, Wickers. He's going to be all right."

17

The Mysterious K.K.

But Odie's grandfather was not all right. He hadn't broken any bones, but eight days later, he was still not home. He had to stay in Bear Falls for special therapy on his back and legs. In the meantime, Kiff and Josie, Odie and Remington tried to keep up the work on the farm.

Odie was worried. "My mom wants to sell the place," he told them. "She says this proves Granddad is too old to be working out here. She wants to get rid of all the horses..." Odie stopped, his face red with feeling.

All four of them were quiet, looking around the peaceful, sweet-smelling barn. What would they do without the old farm? Kiff ruffled Efstur's glimmering forelock. "Don't worry," he muttered. "We'll think of something."

"The main thing," Josie said, "is to prove we can look after the horses by ourselves. C'mon, let's get to work."

"The *main* thing," Kiff said in Odie's ear, "is to find out what my gold is worth. I might be able to buy the whole farm! My dad's going to Bear Falls for supplies tomorrow. I'm going to go with him and check on my rock sample. That geologist must have an answer by now!"

The next morning, there was a different person behind the counter of the mining office.

"You must be the mysterious K.K." The man cocked a sarcastic eyebrow at Kiff. "Where did you say you found this sample?"

"I didn't say," Kiff told him.

"Did you pick it up from someone's collection? Or maybe at a rock display in a museum, by any chance...?" The man's eyes were cold behind his mocking voice.

Kiff was excited and insulted at the same time. The rock sample was valuable all right — valuable enough to be in a museum display! But they didn't believe he'd found it. They thought he'd stolen it! He'd tell them! "I found it..." he started to say, and then realized it probably was a trick to get him to tell just where he *had* found it.

HOW STUPID DO THEY THINK I AM! He took a deep breath and tried to control his anger. "I'd like my sample back now!"

"I'm sorry, but we're not finished running our tests on it yet, K.K." The geologist didn't sound sorry!

"When will you be finished?" Kiff managed to get out between clenched teeth.

"A few days. Don't worry. We'll keep it safe." The man leaned over the counter with a fake friendly smile. One side of his mouth went up. The other went down. He looked like a sick dog. "I'd suggest you tell an adult all about this...'find' of yours," he told Kiff. "That would be better for everybody, don't you think?"

In a few days, Kiff thought, that gold will be under so much muck and water, we won't be able to find it! Why didn't adults ever take him seriously? He banged the door of the mining office to express his feelings and tore down the street to the town dock. There was still one adult who listened to him. His dad was loading supplies on the big *Queen*.

Kiff picked up a heavy carton of canned beans and handed it to his father. "Dad," he started, "I've got something important to tell you." His father looked up. "It's nothing bad," Kiff said quickly. "I found a rock with lots of gold in it. I took it to the mining office, but they keep stalling with the results. And the beaver pond is flooding the cave where I found the gold, and..."

"Another gold rock?" His dad laughed. He put down the stack of cartons he was loading. "You didn't really take it to the mining office..."

He shook his head. "Kiff, that rock belongs with the other nine hundred and ninety-nine gold rocks in your room. You shouldn't bother the government geologists."

Kiff stifled a wild urge to shove his father into Big Pickle Lake. "You won't be laughing when my mine is churning out gold bricks worth millions!" he shouted.

"Listen, Kiff," his dad quit laughing and sat down on the stack of boxes, "I pray to God there never is another gold mine around here. Do you know what it would do to a place like this?" He gestured around the quiet lakefront scene.

"I worked in mining towns all over the north, before we bought the camp. I never want to live near one again." He ruffled Kiff's brown hair. "So if you ever do find gold, keep it quiet."

WHAT WAS THE MATTER WITH EVERY-BODY! "I...you..." Kiff stammered, "Dad, don't you want to own a gold mine? Don't you want to be rich?"

"People like us don't own gold mines." His dad had started loading boxes again. "Bankers own gold mines. Giant corporations own gold mines. And they get rich. People like us just get the garbage that's left over. We get the bad air, the lung disease, the poisoned water and soil. The bankers get it too, but they have bottled water and air purifiers."

"STOP!" Kiff said. "I get the point." They were all against him — his father, Odie's grandfather, and even Odie, his so-called friend! Kiff knew Odie hadn't really believed him about the gold. And with his cave full of water, it was no wonder. He just had to keep on believing himself and wait for the results of the assay. Kiff untied the rope of the *Queen* and jumped aboard. In the meantime, Kiff thought, I just hope the beaver pond doesn't get so deep I never find my cave again!

By the time Kiff got back from Bear Falls, work at the farm was almost finished for the afternoon. The stalls were mucked out, the horses fed, groomed, and watered.

Josie shot daggers at him with her eyes. "Where were you all day, Kokatow?"

"I had to help my dad," Kiff said. "You guys have done a great job here. Now that you're all done, why don't we take the horses out for a ride?"

The others all looked at each other. "I guess Granddad wouldn't mind if we took them out," Odie said slowly.

"It's been more than a week since they had any *real* exercise," Josie added. "But if we're going, we should get started." She pointed at big black clouds that were racing in from the east. "It looks like we might get a storm later."

"I guess I should ride Smoke," Kiff said. "Her leg must be better by now!"

"NO!" Remington said, with a flash of his old stubborn self.

Kiff stared at him. "What do you mean 'No'?" Remington had been so meek and quiet lately, you almost forgot he was there.

"Odie's granddad said Smoke needed more time...the day he got hurt," Remington blurted.

"Okay," Kiff agreed quickly. "I'll ride Ef." He didn't mind. He and the little horse seemed to have a bond. They both loved to run hard and take risks. Ef could have been a warrior's horse in a sci-fi story, Kiff thought. He was the sort of partner you could count on when things got tough.

"Know where I'd like to go?" he asked the others.

"We don't always have to go where *you* want," Josie was buckling Skydive's chin strap.

Kiff shrugged, "Sure. It's not my fault that I usually have all the good ideas."

"And all the bad ones!" Josie shot back.

Kiff ignored her. "I'd still like to ride Efstur on the Red Slimes," he said. "Up at the far end, where they're nice and wide. We can go for a good gallop..."

"Near the riding camp?" Odie interrupted. "We'll never get that far before the storm."

"We don't have to go as far as Camp Saddlemore," Kiff said. "We'll just go to the other side of the beaver pond and then cut back to the slimes." He nodded at Josie.

"As long as you promise not to dive off your horse and attack the beavers with your bare hands," Josie laughed. "You know it's useless, anyhow."

Kiff held up his hand. "I solemnly promise not to disturb our furry little friends." Josie was right, after all. One person couldn't do much against a determined gang of beavers. But at least he could check on the pond.

"Okay." Josie gave her saddle a final tug. "Let's get going."

"We'll have to leave Remington by himself," Odie said. They all stopped and looked at Remington.

"I'll be all right," he said. "Go!"

18

Remington Tries

Remington hadn't realized, until they rode away, how lonesome it would be at the farm by himself. How empty it would feel without Odie's grandfather. He stood leaning on the pasture fence, remembering their lessons together.

"Show them...show them what you can do." Odie's grandfather's voice seemed to ring in his ears. But even if he had the nerve to ride Smoke by himself, Remington thought, then they would all know how he had let Mr. Pedersen down. They'd realize he could have ridden for help — and didn't.

Smoke came over to the pasture fence and thrust her warm nose into his hand. Remington felt a huge lump in his throat. He didn't belong here. Or at Camp Kokatow. Nobody really wanted him at Kiff's place.

Smoke nudged him again, hoping for carrots. The only place I belong, Remington thought, is Camp Saddlemore. At least there, my parents paid for me. Thousands of dollars of camp fees, wasted. It would be enough money to buy Smoke's hay for a whole year!

Remington suddenly knew what he was going to do. "Come on, Smoke," he said. He led her into the barn. Bridle, saddle, get her ready to ride the way Odie's grandfather had taught him.

"I'm going back," he told Smoke. "If the Mountjoys, and the counsellors, and the other Raccoons don't like it ...tough!"

Camp Saddlemore would have to take him back. He'd paid. Remington knew he had to hurry if he didn't want to meet the others coming back. With any luck, they would still be galloping over the Red Slimes when he passed by on the way to camp. He led Smoke out into the yard. The clouds had covered the sun, and thunder was rumbling in the distance. The afternoon seemed very dark after so many days of sunshine. It made Remington shiver. He wasn't sure if he was cold, or just scared.

"Okay, Smoke," he said. "It's just you and me." He took a deep breath, raised his left foot into the stirrup, and swung his right leg over Smoke's back. There! He was sitting in the saddle. Now if he could just make Smoke go in the direction he wanted her to go...He gave her a gentle nudge with his heels and clucked his tongue.

Smoke whinnied and looked over her shoulder at him. Then she started up the familiar trail out of the farmyard and into the trees, at a slow walk. Remington leaned forward and patted her neck. "Good girl," he said. "I hope you're going to like horse camp."

Maybe Kiff would let him keep Smoke till his parents got back, he thought. Maybe he'd even trade horses, period. But no, Remington remembered sadly. His parents would never go for it. Efstur was too "valuable." Remington was really beginning to hate that word.

Far ahead, the others had reached the slimes.

"Let's go!" Kiff's shout was blown back to Josie on the wind. She watched Efstur shoot off as though his legs were springs. He joined Odie and Dinah racing down a finger of flat red sand. Josie hung back. Skydive was nervous, as though he could smell the storm coming. But it wasn't just that. Something was bothering Josie, too. She knew the way the wilderness should look. It was as familiar to her as her own bedroom. Today, something was out of place...

A strong gust of wind blew Skydive's pale mane across his eyes. Josie suddenly missed her own long hair, blowing across her face, the way it always used to, before she had it cut.

All at once, Josie knew what was wrong. On a day as windy as this, there should be clouds of red dust in the air. Why wasn't the red sand blowing? Josie wanted to call out a warning to

Odie and Kiff, but the wind whipped the words out of her mouth. She urged Skydive forward.

Something else was wrong! The horses in front of her were leaving deep tracks in the slimes. Usually their tracks disappeared almost immediately on the hard-packed surface. But now, Josie could see two sets of hoofprints as distinct as if they were running in soft mud.

"STOP!" Josie screamed, but it was too late. A high panicked whinny drowned out her voice. Josie saw Dinah fall to her knees.

Kiff whirled around on Efstur. He galloped back hard towards her. "Odie's broken through," he roared. "Dinah's stuck."

They could hear Dinah's horrible screams of panic as she struggled in the sucking mud. They could see Odie, off her back now, fighting to control Dinah's plunging, heaving body.

"Quick! Get the horses off the slimes," Kiff cried. "It's like quicksand out there!" He rode Ef up into the trees, threw himself off his back and quickly lashed his reins around a small pine.

"The beaver pond," Josie tied Skydive nearby. "It must be backing up into the slimes."

Kiff's eyes were scared. "It must have been flooding all summer. It's horrible out there. We've got to help Odie...before he gets in too deep! Come on." Kiff started running back onto the red sand.

"I'm right behind you." Josie snatched up a stout cedar pole from an old fence and raced after Kiff. There was no time to lose! The rain had started to fall, and that would not help. Every step, her boots sank a little deeper in the thick red sludge. By the time they reached Odie, he had sunk to his knees and was in danger from Dinah's wildly thrashing body. Dinah was terrified. Her frantic heaves would work one foot out, only to have it stuck again.

"Don't come any closer," Odie shouted, when they were a few metres away. "You'll just get stuck too!" He kept trying to reach Dinah's halter, to grab her and quiet her. "If I can't keep her quiet, she'll break her legs," Odie screamed.

Josie threw her cedar pole across the red mud to him. "Odie," she cried. "Lay the stick flat across the slimes. Try to use it to keep yourself up!" The danger was more than broken legs, she thought. The danger was that they would keep on sinking! In some places, the slimes were deeper than a two-storey building.

Odie shook his head. "I can't move my legs...I can't reach ..."

"I've got to help him," Kiff suddenly shouted, snatching up the cedar pole and plunging forward.

"NO, KIFF, DON'T!" Josie yelled, but it was too late. Kiff was lunging towards Odie and the horse. A few more steps and he was stuck tight, with the pole held just out of reach of Odie's outstretched hand.

19

Race to Camp Saddlemore

As Remington got near the Red Slimes, it suddenly started to rain hard. Large drops splattered on Smoke's face and made her shake her head. "Easy, girl," Remington soothed. "It's just water."

He heard the shouting from the slimes before he saw Josie and the others. Then a high whinny of terror made Smoke jump and snort with fear. She burst into a jerky trot. Remington clutched hard with his knees, trying to remember Odie's grandfather's instructions for staying in the saddle.

Around the next bend, he saw the whole picture through a curtain of pelting rain. Odie and Kiff were fighting with a plunging horse out on the Red Slimes. Josie was running towards him, but moving as if she were in a nightmare, as though her feet were stuck to the ground. She was gasping for breath as she reached the edge of the red mud. Her boots were cased in huge blobs of dark red muck.

"Remington!" She stared at him as if he were a vision in her dream. "How did you... Never mind! Am I glad to see you!"

Smoke was prancing and shaking with fear. Josie reached up and grabbed her bridle with a firm hand. "The boys and Dinah are sinking!" she panted, as she tied Smoke near the other horses. "We have to find more planks ... to keep them from sink..."

Josie never finished her sentence. They heard a grinding, cracking boom in the distance, a sound like a huge creaking door being flung open.

"What...?" Remington stared.

"Something's happening...to the slimes," Josie's voice was harsh and urgent. She gazed out across the sea of red mud. "I think the old earth dam must be giving way, down at the end."

The sound was growing, booming and roaring and echoing off the surrounding forest. "All this weight of muck and water must be leaning on the dam..." Josie's face was pale, and her dark eyes looked almost black as she turned to Remington. "The riding camp! If the dam bursts, it will get buried under the slimes!" She and Remington stared at each other.

"HE..LP!" Kiff was bellowing over the noise. "Bring us some more planks. We're going down like the *Titanic* out here!"

"I'm coming," Josie bellowed back. "Listen Remington..." She grabbed his arm. "Ride to the camp, warn them. And then bring back lots of rope and help!"

"You'd better go," Remington begged. "Look at Smoke!" By now, Smoke was badly spooked. She rolled her eyes and snorted with terror. Remington knew he could not get on her back again.

"I have to stay and help Kiff and Odie. Just go! And hurry!" Josie shouted over her shoulder. She was already dragging a large cedar plank down to the edge of the slimes.

"I CAN'T!" Remington waved his arms and jumped from one foot to the other, but it was no use. Josie was leaving. She was counting on him. Remington felt a kind of reckless giddiness rise up inside him. Okay, he would have to take Skydive. But Josie's horse snorted in alarm when Remington went near, stomping and straining at the reins that held him to the tree. Forget Skydive.

There was only one horse left. Remington glanced over at Efstur, quietly munching grass under a tree in the pouring rain. Ef was calm as a cucumber. At that moment, he looked up and shook a shower of raindrops off his frizzled forelock, as if to say, "What are we waiting for?"

"Okay." Remington brushed back the hair that was plastered to his own forehead, dripping into his eyes. "I'll try." Before he could think about it, Remington whipped the reins off the tree and thrust his foot in the stirrup.

"I'm the boss, I'm the boss." He landed softly but firmly in Ef's saddle. "Just remember, Efstur. You're the best, but I'm the boss!

"And don't go too fast," he added, as they swung back on the trail. "I never got past the trot lesson!" Whatever Ef was doing, it was sure faster than a trot. Remington just prayed he could hang on until they got to the camp.

He kept along the edge of the slimes, so he wouldn't get lost. In places, the thick red mud had buried the trail and Remington depended on Ef's sure feet to find his way up and down over the rocks and around the tangles of brush in their way.

When they reached the part where the Red Slimes narrowed, Remington saw something that made him suck in his breath with horror.

Through the pouring rain he could see a channel opening in the centre of the slimes, a crack like in an earthquake movie he'd watched on TV. Only this wasn't TV. This was real! Red sludge was flowing down into the deep chasm, causing smaller cracks to appear all across the surface of the slimes.

"C'mon, Ef," he urged, but the little Icelandic horse didn't need any extra urging. He seemed to understand that this was an important mission. Sure-footed and quick, he was picking up the signals from Remington's hands as though he'd thought of them first.

They were almost at the old earth dam overlooking Camp Saddlemore. Remington gave Ef a nudge and he surged forward to the edge. There he stopped short, tossing his shaggy head and whinnying in alarm. Remington dashed the rain out of his eyes. He could hardly believe what he was seeing. The whole dam was caving in. In the centre, a thick river of red mud slid through a gap as high as a house.

The slimes mud moved like heavy syrup, snapping off tree trunks as if they were straws. It buried bushes, rocks, small trees in its path. In just a few moments it would break through the final screen of trees and begin to bury the camp.

Unbelievably, Camp Saddlemore seemed to have no idea of the wall of mud that was sliding towards them. In a quick glance, Remington saw no horses, no people — anywhere. Everybody must be inside...out of the storm.

"Let's go, Efstur!" With a wild shout, Remington urged Ef down through the trees at the side of the dam, through the thin band of pines and into the camp.

"GET THE HORSES OUT OF HERE! SOMEBODY! COME QUICK!" he roared. He galloped up to the camp's main office. Somebody must be here! Remington threw himself off Ef's back and dashed inside.

"Mr. Wickers!" Mr. Mountjoy looked up from his bookkeeping with a startled face. "DON'T

YOU KNOW THIS IS REST HOUR? ALL CAMPERS MUST BE IN THEIR BUNKS FOR A FULL HOUR..."

"I'm not a camper," Remington gasped. "And by the end of rest hour, you're going to be buried six-feet deep in Red Slimes if you don't do something quick."

Mr. Mountjoy put his hand down firmly on the telephone, as Remington grabbed for it. "That's correct, you are no longer a camper. How did you get here? No, never mind how you got here. Just leave!" Mr. Mountjoy blustered.

"You brainless old toot!" Remington screamed. "I'm not leaving! I came to save your stupid camp! Why don't you listen to me? Why don't you just go out and look for yourself, if you don't believe me?"

Mr. Mountjoy started to his feet, his face purple with rage.

At the same moment, the door banged open, and the Raccoon counsellor came puffing in. "Mr. Mountjoy. There's something strange happening in the woods," he panted. "I saw it from the hayloft in the barn. Trees are falling down..."

Mr. Mountjoy gave one last startled glance at Remington and then bustled after the counsellor. Remington turned to follow them and then thought of the telephone. He picked it up and dialled — not 911, but 0 for operator. Somebody had to answer!

20

Stuck in the Muck

Josie's words rang in Remington's ears. BRING ROPE, LOTS OF IT! And help, she'd said. There was no telling when help might arrive, but he could bring the rope. He and Efstur. He grabbed Efstur's reins and ran for the main barn where rope was stored.

Camp Saddlemore was a scene of mass confusion. Campers, clutching armloads of their favourite clothes, pictures and riding gear, struggled out of their bunkhouses. Mr. and Mrs. Mountjoy dashed in all directions, screeching useless orders.

Remington left it all behind without a backwards glance. As they reached the trail, Efstur picked up speed. He didn't seem to mind the coils of rope flapping at his side. Remington could hardly believe this was the same horse that had jerked and jolted him around the show ring. Ef was running with a smooth, effortless pace. It felt to Remington like they were flying.

But the trail was full of dangers. Fingers of red mud, and streams of water had almost washed it out completely. They had to make a new trail through the brush and trees. Efstur hardly even paused. He splashed through water and plunged through thick woods as though breaking trail was the easiest thing in the world.

Remington remembered how Odie's grandfather had described the Icelandic horses fording rivers of frigid water in Iceland. No wonder Efstur felt at home in the northern wilderness.

Half an hour later, they were in sight of Josie and the others. "I'm back," Remington shouted. "I brought rope..." He stopped, trying to take in what was happening.

Out on the slimes, half-a-football-field away, Kiff and Odie were flopped on the old planks, trying to wriggle their legs out of the thick slimes mud.

"I think I've got my toes free," he heard Kiff shout. "Hey! There's Wickers!"

Josie leaped to her feet and hopscotched back toward Remington on the plank pathway she had made. "Throw me the rope," she cried. "You're just in time."

Remington ran out as far as he dared and pitched Josie one end of a long coil of rope.

"Tie the other end to Ef's saddle!" she called. "Okay, you two. Who's first?" She threw Odie the rope, and he tied it in a slipknot under his armpits.

"Are you ready to pull?" Josie shouted back to Remington.

"RIGHT." He had knotted the rope firmly to Efstur's saddle. When Josie gave the signal, he urged Ef to pull. Once more the little horse tossed his mane and strained forward. He seemed to know exactly what to do. Odie's granddad had said horses from Iceland had been sent to pull heavy carts full of coal through dark mine tunnels in Britain. Even though Ef was small, he was incredibly strong.

"WHOA. WAIT. HEY!"

Remington turned to see Odie pop free and flop across the surface of the slimes like a hooked fish.

"Okay, Ef," Remington signalled. "That's one. Now Kiff Kokatow..."

Kiff tied the rope under his arms. Another mighty effort from Efstur, and Kiff came slipping across the slimes with bare feet. The red muck had claimed his riding boots.

Both Kiff and Odie were caked with slimes. "I can't wait to wash this sludge off," Kiff groaned."I feel like all those chemicals are eating through my skin." They staggered up to the shelter of the trees. The rain had almost stopped, but a haze of grey drizzle still hung over the slimes.

"I'm sure sorry to lose those boots..." Kiff started.

"What about Dinah!" Odie interrupted. "We've got to get her out of there!" He peered through the thickening fog, trying to see his horse more clearly.

"We'll need help to pry her loose." Kiff shook his head. "Not even Efstur could yank her out of that crazy glue!" He turned to Remington. "Did you say help was coming?"

"I don't know...I couldn't tell if I made them understand on the phone what was happening..." Remington faltered. "I tried, but no one seemed to care about a slimes dam breaking. Maybe the operator was just a recorded message."

"I bet those beavers are having a good laugh, eh Moonster?" Kiff groaned. "This must be the best rodent joke of the century...'Did you hear the one about how we built a *really big* dam and flooded the whole slimes?' HA!"

"Kiff, I'm sorry. We should have listened to you about the beavers."

"Well, don't worry. There are lots of people at Camp Saddlemore," Kiff said. "Somebody will come, right Remington?"

"I don't know..." Remington said again. He described the frantic scene he had left behind at the camp — adults and campers running in all directions, the wall of Red Slimes mud slowly burying the camp as it slid towards the lakeshore...

All at once Kiff Kokatow's face grew pale under its streaks of red mud. He turned horrified eyes to Josie. "The lake!" he shouted. "The slimes are spilling into the lake!"

They all stared at him.

"Don't you see?" Kiff waved his arms wildly. "All this...tons and tons of poisoned mud is flowing into Big Pickle Lake!"

"It will poison the water," Josie gasped. "Kill all the fish...the animals..."

"The town drinking water, our fishing camp — it'll all be dead as a doornail once the slimes hit the water. We've got to do something..." Kiff was already in action. "Odie, I promise, we'll send some help for Dinah as soon as we get to town."

He glanced at the horses. "I'll ride Smoke. Come on, Remington, you're doing great on Efstur!" He stopped for a second, and stared at Remington. "How on earth did you learn to ride like that? Never mind, tell me later!"

He threw his wet and slippery body onto Smoke's saddle. "Go ahead!" he shouted. "You and Ef can probably go faster."

"I'll stay and help get some ropes around Dinah," Josie said. "Oh, go quick," she added, glancing up at Kiff's mud-streaked face. They both knew what could happen to the lake if they didn't stop the slimes!

21

Stop the Slimes!

Kiff rode Smoke like a red demon. In his mind, he could see the wall of slimes, oozing closer to the lake every second. He felt as though he was riding for the life of Big Pickle Lake and all the creatures who lived in it and on its shores.

Ahead, on Efstur, Remington's body crouched forward as they flew down the trail.

Past the beaver dam they rode, up and over the old Carter Mine hill. The going was harder here. Efstur was much more sure-footed than Smoke on the broken rock and deep ruts.

"Go ahead!" Kiff yelled. "Head for the Post Office in town. I'll meet you there."

Soon, Remington and Efstur were out of sight. Kiff pressed on. The rain had stopped, and he could feel the wind rushing past drying the mud on his body into a hard shell. When he reached the main road, Kiff urged Smoke into a fast canter, praying that no logging trucks would come speeding down the hill into town behind him. As he rode up the main street, he saw Efstur tied to a signpost in front of the Post Office. Remington must already be inside. Kiff flung himself off Smoke's back and dashed up the Post Office steps. Through the glass door, he could see Remington pounding on the counter in frustration.

"SLIMES!" he heard him bellow, as he burst through the doors. "CAVE IN!"

Mrs. Duke, who ran the Post Office, was shaking her head and glaring at Remington. "Stop pounding on my counter, young man, and calm down!"

"Mrs. Duke, listen! The slimes have broken through the dam," Kiff croaked, through the mask of mud on his face. "They're running into the lake up at Camp Saddlemore. The whole thing's going to slide into the lake and poison the water and..."

"Good grief! Kiff Kokatow, is that you?" Mrs. Duke's mouth hung open in shock. "What have you done to yourself?"

"It's like someone popped the cap on a big tube of toothpaste!" Remington cried. "And this red gook is all oozing out." He held up Kiff's mud-caked arm to demonstrate.

"Can we use your phone, Mrs. Duke?" Kiff asked. "We need to call the police and the Department of Mines. We need bulldozers and trucks and..."

"Helicopters," Remington suggested. "To rescue Dinah and Odie."

"Right. Helicopters. Remington, you are a genius."

Kiff reached for the telephone Mrs. Duke pushed across the counter. At last someone was listening to him. If it took getting slimed, it was worth it!

Within an hour, a rescue helicopter hovered over the slimes where Dinah was still imprisoned in the thick red mud. Odie, wrapped in a warm blanket, watched from the edge as a sling was lowered and fastened under Dinah's belly. Gently she was lifted out of the mud and set down on safe, firm ground.

"She can't stand up!" Odie cried, as Dinah's legs crumpled under her.

"We'll get a vet up here in a four-by-four," the rescue worker said. "In the meantime, get the horse dry and keep her warm, if you can..." He looked doubtfully at the four exhausted kids. "Anybody want a helicopter ride back to town?"

"No...we've got our horses," Kiff said. "Unless you want to go, Remington."

Remington looked at the helicopter pilot and the shiny silver-and-red machine. He looked at Efstur. He supposed they'd have to go and get horse blankets and stuff, and then ride back here, and then... His body felt one hundred years old after all the riding he'd done today...

"No," he finally heard himself say. "I guess I'll stay with these guys."

Kiff grinned, as the helicopter pilot strode away to his machine. "Way to go, Wickers. I can't believe the way you rode today. Now, tell us how you did it...and start from the beginning!"

22

Beavers and Mr. Mountjoy

All night workers and equipment fought a huge battle to keep the slimes from spilling into Big Pickle Lake. While Kiff and Odie, Josie and Remington slept an exhausted sleep, bulldozers dug huge ditches to divert the slimes mud away from the lake. Trucks rumbled down to Camp Saddlemore carrying tons of rock and gravel to build a new dam to stop the flow. A hole was punched in the beaver dam, and the water drained out through Licking Creek.

By morning no one would have recognized Camp Saddlemore. The paddocks and riding ring were deep in red slimes. All that was left were a few bunkhouses and the rounded tops of horse vans sticking up through the ooze.

By the time Kiff and Remington arrived that afternoon, all the campers and their horses had gone. The clean-up crew was surrounding what was left of the camp with bright orange fencing and hanging warning signs on it.

"DANGER, KEEP OUT," Kiff read. "As if anyone would want to go in." They were standing on the other side of the fence, looking in at the disaster.

"I guess your parents would have ended up with me anyway," Remington sighed, "after this…"

"I guess so," Kiff grinned. "Look. There's old Mountjoy."

On the other side of the fence, an angry Mr. Mountjoy was having a loud argument with a government official in a hard hat. "I don't know how this could have happened," he bellowed. "Don't you people up here look after your dams and things?"

"Let's go closer and listen," Kiff said. They worked their way along the fence until they were right behind the furious camp director's broad back.

The Ministry official was consulting his clipboard. "I believe you are the owner of this property, sir?" he asked.

"That's right," Mr. Mountjoy's padded shoulders rose. "And what I'd like to know is…"

"Then that's *your* waste pond that just burst its dam," the official said calmly. "And your slimes that are pouring into the environment. I'm afraid you may be in for a hefty bill for part of this clean up."

"What? A BILL! Well, I never heard of such a thing…. You mean that all this mud…?"

"That's right, sir. These are your slimes."

Kiff and Remington turned and ran. They got as far as they could before they collapsed with helpless laughter.

"I wish I could have seen his face," Kiff howled with glee.

"I hope he has to pay for it all," Remington held his aching sides. "I hope they make him clean up the whole lake!" He stopped laughing and looked at Kiff. "They are going to be able to clean it up, aren't they?"

"My dad says it will be months before we really know," Kiff's face got serious too. "We'll have to keep testing the water and see if the fish get sick…"

"All because of Mrs. Mountjoy's grandfather and a bunch of beavers," Remington shook his head. "What's going to happen to the beavers?"

"They've probably given up, now their dam is destroyed," Kiff said. "We should ride up there this afternoon and see."

They found Josie Moon sitting alone beside the half-empty beaver pond. Odie was at home in town. His grandfather was out of the hospital at last, but still walking with a cane.

Kiff and Remington left their horses near Dinah and slid down the bank beside Josie.

"What are you doing up here, Moonbrain?" Kiff asked.

"Well, I was watching the beavers fix their dam, until you two came along and scared them away. Look, Kiff, it's half-built up again."

Kiff was astonished. "What does it take to discourage these guys?"

"My dad says the wildlife officers are going to live-trap them and move them away from the slimes," Josie grinned. "They'll just start again somewhere else. Hey, Remington! How's the hero today?"

Remington sat down awkwardly. His legs were still stiff from all of yesterday's hard riding. He ignored Josie's "hero" remark. "You were right, Kiff," he said. "There *are* too many beavers in this world."

"I was starting to agree with you," Josie sighed, "but I've been up here, watching, all morning."

"Watching a bunch of animal over-achievers wreck the environment." Kiff chucked a stone in the quiet pond.

"Stop that, Kokatow, and listen."

They were all quiet for a minute.

"Lots of mosquitoes," Remington said.

"Lots of birds, too. I saw a Great Blue heron fishing, and there are ducks, and a hawk perched on that tallest dead tree," Josie said. "And muskrats had a home under this bank, and there are deer tracks and moose tracks, and hundreds of frogs, and minnows in the water…"

"And millions of mosquitoes," Kiff slapped one that had landed on his neck. "*Great* place for them to breed! A nice big scummy green swamp!"

"Okay, it might look like a mess to us, but this is really beautiful, if you're a bird, or an animal!" Josie protested. "The beavers created a whole world for all these other guys..."

"And in the process, flooded the slimes and almost wrecked our lake!" Kiff shouted.

"It wasn't their fault the gold mine left their poison muck just sitting in the bush for thirty years!" Josie was getting mad. "You're an environmental meathead, Kokatow!"

They glared at each other for a moment. "Remind me," Kiff suddenly stood up, "that once this pond is drained, there's something up near the mine I want to show Wickers before he leaves."

"You're leaving, Remington?" Josie looked up at him quickly.

Remington frowned. "My parents get back from the Rain Forest tomorrow," he said glumly.

"They'll be proud to hear about how you saved the camp and rode to town and got a helicopter to pull Dinah out..."

"They won't care unless there's a gold medal involved," Remington sighed. "They have this thing about winning prizes!"

23

Norse Horse Expert

For his last breakfast at Camp Kokatow, Remington had something of his own to show Kiff.

"It's my new system for making toast," he told Kiff proudly. "See, I lay eight pieces of bread out at a time — right on top of the wood stove," he demonstrated. "Then I flip them in about a minute and a half. The ones nearest the fire box are ready first. I butter those, and by that time, the other ones are ready."

Remington looked like he had eight arms, buttering, stacking and flipping toast. About every sixth slice hit the floor. Miska and Tiska sat close by the stove to catch them. They looked at Remington with adoration in their eyes.

"Delicious breakfast," one of the guests popped his head into the kitchen to say. "Loved the toast — nice and crunchy."

Kiff laughed. "This could totally revolutionize camp breakfast, Wickers."

"Thanks," Remington beamed. He hauled eight more slices from the bread bag and slapped them on the hot stove. "Hey, Kiff, do you think your parents might need help...again next summer? I could come back, and work in the kitchen."

Kiff was saved from answering by a signal from the mainland.

HONK!...HONK!...HONK!

The Wickers were back.

Half an hour later, Remington's parents were climbing up the path to the main lodge. They looked exhausted. His father had a peeling sunburn, and his mother's hair had lost its shiny glaze. It stuck out from her head in tufts, like old doll's hair.

"So," Mr. Wickers puffed, "I guess the riding camp didn't turn out so well, eh Son?" He sighed as he plopped down in one of the camp's comfortable armchairs beside the fireplace. "We got all the fax messages when I checked in at the office."

"Sorry about the faxes, Dad," Remington said. "How was the Rain Forest?"

"Well, Marge and I certainly had our eyes opened, didn't we, hon?"

"Ohhh!" Mrs. Wickers fluttered her hands. "We certainly did. The food was *nothing* like they promised. Your father had stomach problems from the first day! We got robbed, and the shopping was terrible! We hardly brought anything home."

"...like I said in the beginning, we should have stayed right here for our holiday, and fished." Mr. Wickers patted the arms of his chair and sighed. "I don't suppose you'd happen to have a piece of that blueberry pie around..." he looked hopefully at the kitchen door as if a blueberry pie might come sailing through it. "I dreamed about Camp Kokatow blueberry pie up and down all the steps of all those ruins in the Rain Forest!"

"The blueberries weren't much good this year..." Kiff's mother was trying not to laugh.

"But we picked tons of raspberries," Remington broke in. "You should taste the raspberry pie, Dad. It's even better. Can I get him a piece?" he looked at Mrs. Kokatow hopefully.

"Sure. Bring us all a piece," Kiff's dad said.

"You, Remington...in the *kitchen?*" Mrs. Wickers looked startled.

"Yup, I've been making toast, washing dishes...everything," Remington shouted from the other room. "And I want to come back and work here next summer."

"Oh, I'm sure we can find a more suitable place..." Mrs. Wickers started to say.

"*This* suits me," Remington came back carrying six pieces of pie on a tray. "You're not dumping me at a stupid horse camp again!" He had drips of raspberry juice down his white shirt and was tracking sticky red juice across the camp floor.

"That's my boy!" Mr. Wickers beamed. "He knows what he likes. Me too. We'll all come back next summer — stay a whole month. Marge, you can go to the Galapagos Islands, if you want. When we Wickers make up our minds, that's about it." He took a big mouthful of pie and munched in perfect contentment for a moment.

"So, Dad, I want to talk to you about Efstur, and riding," Remington said firmly. It wasn't often he caught his parents at such a weak moment. He was going to take advantage of this one.

"Sorry the horse didn't work out either," Mr. Wickers mumbled. "S'ppose we could sell him..."

"I have a better idea," Remington said, "when you've finished your pie."

When they had all finished, Remington insisted that his parents get back in the big *Queen*, pick up their truck and horse van at the landing, and drive to Odie's farm. Odie and Josie were already there, catching up on work in the barn.

Odie's grandfather came out to meet them. He had lost weight and needed the cane to walk. But the sparkle was back in his eyes. He was very happy to see Remington.

"I hear that you and the little Icelander have been having some adventures while I was away," he grinned.

"I guess so," Remington smiled back. "Ef was amazing, Mr. Pedersen. He just flew over that rough trail."

"Your son is a very good rider," Olaf Pedersen said, turning to Remington's parents. "He has hands like silk."

Mr. and Mrs. Wickers stared at Remington's hands.

"Odie's grandfather taught me how to ride," Remington explained. "He's a Norse horse expert."

"A what...?" Mr. Wickers looked confused.

"He comes from Sweden. A long time ago, they had horses like Efstur. They're very special. The Norse gods, Odin and Thor rode them in the sagas. Mr. Pedersen says Ef needs to live in a place where he can get outside in the winter and get toughened up, and eat grass and run free. *He* says Ef might pine away and die if we keep him down south in a heated barn all the time." Remington paused to take a breath.

"Is that so?" Mr. Wickers was interested. "Well, he is a very *valuable* piece of horseflesh!"

"...and *also*," Remington plunged ahead, "Mr. Pedersen says Ef needs company — other horses to hang around with. And he really likes the horses here, Smoke, and Dinah, and Skydive. He hated those Camp Saddleburn horses."

"Saddle*burn*?" Mrs. Wickers frowned.

"That's what Kiff calls it," Remington grinned. "And he's right, Mother. They may be the best people, but they don't know beans about riding!"

"Well, I can see Efstur likes it here." Mr. Wickers looked thoughtfully at the horses grazing in the pasture. Dinah was still recovering in her stall from the ordeal in the slimes.

"So I think," Remington finished in a gust, "we should board Ef here all year and pay Mr. Pedersen lots of money, because he's a real expert at looking after..."

"Norse horses, eh? Well, of course you have to pay top money to get real expertise," Mr. Wickers was nodding agreement. All of this — the raspberry pie, the thought of spending a month next year fishing, and now a new and interesting way to spend his money — was putting him in a wonderful mood.

Mrs. Wickers was also looking more cheerful. "It would be so *unique*," she sighed, looking around the old farm. "Oh, Remington, dear, what a good idea!"

"Of course, Mr. Pedersen would have to be willing to board your horse." Mr. Wickers looked at Odie's grandfather hopefully.

Now it was Odie's turn to try to keep a straight face. He knew this would give his grandfather a reason to keep the farm running!

"Ya. I think we could manage okay," Odie's grandfather said, after a pause. "We have lots of help from my grandson, and his friends. Sure, we could try it out for a year."

"Then let's say it's a done deal and unhitch this horse van right here and now," Mr. Wickers chuckled. "No use dragging the darned thing back to St. Catharines!"

"Come, Remington," Mrs. Wickers said. "We should go back to Camp Kokatow and collect your things. I'm dying to get home!" She patted her hair.

"Josie Moon will bring me back," Remington said. "I want to take a last ride on Ef. For this year..." he added. He smiled at Kiff. "I guess I got my revenge, Kokatow," he said. "You're going to have to put up with me all next summer."

"I guess I will," Kiff grinned back. "Come on, let's go for that ride. There's something I want to show you before you leave, like I said."

24

The Last Ride

They scrambled down the hill on the other side of the old Carter Mine and slid down Kiff's yellow rope.

"There it is," Kiff said. "There's my cave. It's full of gold!"

"Kiff, I can't believe you are still gold crazy," Josie groaned. "Even after everything that's happened?"

"It's in here..." Kiff bent low and shone the beam of his flashlight on the cave floor. "Of course, the flood covered it up a bit with mud and old leaves."

Josie was still shaking her head. "The last mine took all the gold out of here," she said, "and left us rubble and slimes!"

"It's a mess, all right," Kiff nodded. "So what would you do, if you found this?" He scraped back the mud with a penknife and shone the beam on the glistening vein of quartz.

"WOW!" Remington's eyes were huge.

"Holy cow!" Josie touched the gold streaks with a finger. "That looks like…"

"The real thing?" Kiff said. "It is. I finally got the word from the mining office today. It's gold all right…" He looked up at the cave ceiling. "I don't know how much is here, but the sample I took was twenty-five ounces to a tonne. That's rich."

Josie studied Kiff's face in the streaky light of the cave. "So why aren't you jumping up and down and screaming in usual Kokatow style?" she asked.

"Partly because of what happened to the Red Slimes," Kiff answered. "Whoever has a gold mine these days, has to clean up the mess they make. It won't be just 'grab the treasure' and run.

"And partly…" he grinned the old Kokatow grin, "because this land has already been staked. I checked it out right away. The mining rights were claimed a few years ago. If the people who own it don't keep up the work on the claim, it will go back to the government, when I'm about…seventeen, I figure.

"In the meantime," he shone the light around the cave again, "it's a great place to come and dream. Thanks to you, Remington, old buddy, we can afford the luxury — now Odie's farm is safe for a while."

He took out a rock hammer and broke off a small piece of the gold-rich quartz and handed it to Remington. "I thought you might like a piece to take home."

"But, if my father sees this..." Remington shook his head.

"No problem," Kiff laughed. "Just tell him it's fool's gold. He'd never believe you if you told him it was real anyway. That's one thing I've learned about adults."

"Our secret treasure!" Remington turned the sparkling sample over in his hand.

"What are you going to do when you're seventeen, Kiff, if nobody finds it before then?" Odie asked. "Will you stake the claim?"

Kiff shrugged. "Who knows?" he grinned. "We prospectors never talk about our plans."

Afterword

Last summer, while returning to our beloved island in the Montreal River north of Elk Lake, Ontario, we found part of the road washed out. On either side was a wasteland of red muck and broken trees, with toxic warning signs sticking out of the mud at crazy angles. We learned that an old mine waste pond had burst through its dam and ripped through the forest above the road. Some of the slimes mud had flowed into the river before it could be stopped. There were no children exploring the woods near the slimes dam on the day it burst, but if there had been, they might have seen that the beaver pond was getting dangerously high or discovered that the slimes mud was like quicksand. They might even have given a warning in time to prevent the disaster.

About the author

Sharon Siamon is an editor and a writer. She has published ten children's novels, including *A Horse for Josie Moon* and *Fishing for Trouble*. An enthusiast about horses, Sharon Siamon lives in Brighton, Ontario. She has a summer home in the northern part of the province, where she, her family, and neighbours faced the ecological problems she describes in this book.